Twelve separate books.

All the gorgeous military heroes you can handle.

One UNIFORMLY HOT! mini-series.

Don't miss Mills & Boon® Blaze®'s first twelve-book continuity series, featuring irresistible soldiers from all branches of the armed forces.

Watch for:

THE SOLDIER by Rhonda Nelson
(Special Forces) July 2010

STORM WATCH by Jill Shalvis
(National Guard) August 2010

HER LAST LINE OF DEFENCE
by Marie Donovan
(Green Berets) September 2010

SOLDIER IN CHARGE by Jennifer LaBrecque
(Paratrooper) October 2010

SEALED AND DELIVERED by Jill Monroe
(Navy SEALs) November 2010

CHRISTMAS MALE by Cara Summers
(Military Police) December 2010

Uniformly Hot!
The Few. The Proud. The Sexy as Hell.

Dear Reader,

I've written many heroes in the course of my career, but I don't know that any of them deserve that description more than Lieutenant Colonel Mitch Dugan. There's just something about a man in uniform, one whose purpose is to protect and defend, whose very code of conduct isn't just a set of rules that he lives by, but is inherent in his makeup as a man—and makes a girl stand up and take notice. That sort of mentality sets him apart from your average guy and makes him more…everything. More sexy, more worthy, more noble. And that kind of guy needs a special kind of woman.

What he doesn't need is a free-spirited woman who grabs him and kisses him the first time she sees him, who's dedicated to her own career, who considers herself allergic to the military lifestyle. When photographer Eden Walters shows up to photograph a paratrooper calendar, Mitch discovers there's one thing he hasn't been trained to handle—her!

I love to hear from my readers, so be sure to pop by my website—www.jenniferlabrecque.com—or visit my group blog with fellow friends and authors Vicki Lewis Thompson and Rhonda Nelson at www.thesoapbox queens.com. There's a party in our castle every day.

Happy reading,

Jennifer LaBrecque

SOLDIER IN
CHARGE

BY
JENNIFER LaBRECQUE

MILLS &
BOON

All the characters in this book have no existence outside the imagination of
the author, and have no relation whatsoever to anyone bearing the same name
or names. They are not even distantly inspired by any individual known or
unknown to the author, and all the incidents are pure invention.

First published in Great Britain 2010
Harlequin Mills & Boon Limited,
Eton House, 18-24 Paradise Road, Richmond, Surrey TW9 1SR

© Jennifer LaBrecque 2009
(Original title: *Ripped!*)

ISBN: 978 0 263 88146 2

14-1010

Harlequin Mills & Boon policy is to use papers that are natural, renewable
and recyclable products and made from wood grown in sustainable forests.
The logging and manufacturing processes conform to the legal environmental
regulations of the country of origin.

Printed and bound in Spain
by Litografia Rosés S.A., Barcelona

After a varied career path that included barbecue-joint waitress, corporate numbers cruncher and bug-business maven, **Jennifer LaBrecque** has found her true calling writing contemporary romance. Named 2001 Notable New Author of the Year and 2002 winner of the prestigious Maggie Award for Excellence, she is also a two-time RITA® Award finalist. Jennifer lives in suburban Atlanta.

This book is most gratefully and humbly dedicated to the men and women in our armed forces and to their families. Thank you so very much for your service.

1

"YOU'VE GOT TO DO IT," Eden Walters's best friend, Patti, said. "The calendar is for a good cause—all the proceeds will go to 82nd Airborne families who've lost loved ones in the line of duty. You're the best photographer in the business and you know the military. You've got to do it," she repeated.

This was a no-brainer. Eden settled back in the wrought-iron chair in her courtyard and laughed, "No, I don't, Patti. Your wheedling isn't going to get you anywhere this time, even if you are a professional at it." She was not being talked into photographing a calendar of Army jumpers. Nope. Not her kind of assignment. Just the thought made her tense up. She took a deep breath and consciously relaxed. Patti could find another professional photographer to rope into this one.

Patti added her signature snort to the attendant sounds of a late-summer evening in New Orleans' French Quarter—the burble of Eden's fountain to the left of the table, the restless whisper of a breeze through the potted palm fronds and bougainvillea, the distant float of laughter and music, the occasional whine of mosquitoes punctuating the cicadas endless chorus.

"A professional." Another snort. "You certainly know how to add a touch of glamour to my job, don't you?" They both knew Eden had the utmost respect for Patti's job as a volunteer recruiter for a nonprofit agency. "It's a good thing I love you like the sister I never had…." Patti trailed off, her good humor evident despite her grousing tone, to sip at the pale yellow limoncello, "You made this?"

"Yep. From my very own lemon tree," Eden nodded toward her pride and joy in the corner of the courtyard's brick wall confines, barely discernable in dusk's shadows.

"Delicious. And I can't believe it took me so long to get down here to see you." Patti leaned her head back against the wrought iron chair and offered an approving smile. "This place is so totally you."

Eden grinned. She'd known Patti would love her home. They'd met in sixth grade at the base's middle school in Hawaii, where both their fathers had been stationed and the two girls had become firm, fast friends. They talked once a month and had long ago fallen into the habit of not answering the phone unless they both had at least an hour at their disposal to yak. Eden had e-mailed pictures but it had taken Patti three years to manage a visit. Her money had been as tight as Eden's.

Eden had fallen in love with the vintage Creole town house, circa 1842, from the moment she'd seen its two-story pink façade faced with turquoise shutters and a second-floor iron balcony. It had spoken to her artist's soul, murmured *this is where you belong*. The first-floor parlor had provided the perfect gallery setting for her photographs, with the upstairs serving as her private living quarters. But it was the lemon tree, laden with the most spectacularly large, yellow fruit she'd ever seen, tucked into the back corner of the foun-tained brick courtyard that had sealed the deal for her.

The place was outside her budgeted price range. And even though a building report came back that the place was structurally sound and the wiring and plumbing had been updated post-Katrina, it needed some serious TLC. Her parents, particularly her Briga-dier General father, would have a friggin heart attack— they considered New Orleans lawless and vulnerable to another disaster.

She'd made an offer the next day.

Once again her parents had tagged her as impulsive. She preferred to think of it as instinctive. And yeah, sometimes it got her into trouble—well, maybe a lot of times—and granted she'd had to eat red beans and rice damn near every meal for a year, but it was finally paying off. She and her photography business had blossomed and grown beyond her wildest imagination. It was as if, after years of growing up in the stifling military envi-ronment, she'd finally found a rich, nurturing place to plant her roots. Granted her photography took her all over the world, but she always came home to here.

"Want to play with the tarot cards?" Patti asked half an hour later when they'd finished their lemon-infused vodka. Eden wasn't drunk, she didn't even qualify as bonafide tipsy, but she was definitely relaxed. And tarot cards were the kind of thing you did with a long-standing friend on a summer night in Nawlin's. Plus, Patti seemed to have a gift with the cards. Tomorrow night they were going out for zydeco dancing, but today they'd strolled through all the French Quarter shops and tonight was for catching up.

"Sure. You grab the cards and I'll light the candles." Dusk had yielded to night while they'd talked.

Patti disappeared into the house for the tarot pack she'd bought that afternoon and Eden padded barefoot across the bricks. She always risked stepping on an insect, and she had run across the occasional snake, but it was worth it to feel the sun-warmed bricks against her bare feet. She retrieved the lighter from a water-proof container she kept in the palm's pot and moved around the small courtyard lighting the tiki torches. She paused in the far corner of the yard, across from the lemon tree. For all that she loved the bright sunny spot and the happy yellow fruit, she was equally enamored with the opposite corner, where the sun only reached briefly.

She brushed her toes over the soft moss that carpeted the bricks in this spot. "Hello, handsome," she said softly as she lit the torch, illuminating the worn statue nestled amongst ferns and fragrant banana shrubs.

"Uh, is there someone else here that I don't know about?" Patti asked from behind her.

Eden laughed. "Patti, meet Mercury, Roman messenger of the gods," she said, gesturing toward the moss-covered life-size concrete casting of the nude god with winged feet. For the most part he blended in with his verdant surroundings. "Mercury, meet Patti, who knows and loves me best."

"All righty, then. Hi, Mercury." Patti shook her head. "You know this is just damn weird that we're talking to a statue."

"Hey, he spoke to me first. I found him one day when I was knocking around an antique shop. I turned the corner and there he stood, stopping me in my tracks." Lean face, chiseled lips, sculpted muscles—she'd had to have him.

"I'm guessing you didn't just toss him in your backseat and haul him home."

Laughing again, Eden shook her head. "Two guys, a dolly, and a lift truck and it was still a bitch to get him back here. Isn't he beautiful?"

"How many times have you photographed him?"

Patti knew her too well. "Lots." She'd fired off hundreds of shots. "He's paid for himself many times over. I did a numbered series of him and it sold phenomenally well."

"Good deal." Patti grabbed the lighter and flicked it on. Holding it lower, she cocked her head to one side and peered closer. "His schwing could be a little bigger."

Eden had thought the same thing—all those nicely defined muscles in the arms, chest, abs, ass and legs, but the penis was on the pretty-damn-small side, even for an unaroused state. She'd told herself it was simply a matter of the artist in her objecting to the lack of physical symmetry. Still, she had to tease Patti. "You know, you have an obsession with male genitalia."

"As if you don't. Please tell me when you're fantasizing you give him a better package."

Eden grinned. "Well, yeah." The sixteenth century sculptor could've been way more generous.

Reclaiming the lighter, Eden finished lighting the garden torches. Patti followed. "You know you seriously need to get out more if you're fantasizing about a statue."

"Says you. He's got a better personality than the last couple of guys I met."

Patti giggled. "Idiot."

"For real. Pickings are pretty slim in the man pool." Eden sat back down in the wrought-iron chair and tucked her heels on the edge, bringing her knees to her chest and wrapping her arms around her legs.

"Maybe you're fishing in the wrong pond." Patti began to shuffle the tarot deck.

"Pond? I've fished in every friggin' ocean I've crossed. There was the local guy here who wanted to wear my panties. No thanks. Then there was the guy I met in Canada who turned out to be married. The Asian guy who wanted us to meditate to an orgasm without touching one another." She paused to draw a breath and Patti held up a staying hand.

"Okay. Okay. I gotcha." She cut her eyes in a sly way. "I just offered you a new pond to fish in. Hot paratroopers."

"I'd rather sign up for a lobotomy. Wait. Getting involved with a military guy would be the same thing. I don't think so. Actually, I believe you've lost your mind."

"Far from it. You've just got such a rigid mind-set— guess you get that from your father."

"Kiss my ass." Okay, so Patti had struck a chord. Her career military father only saw things in black and white. It drove Eden crazy. Had always driven her crazy because she was all about shades of gray and Techni-color.

"Think compromise, *liebling*. Think about hard bodies, males in their prime in top-notch condition. Think of hot, sweaty sex. Think about you wrapping up the assignment, and then spending your time anyway you please. I get what I want, which is the best damn photographer in the business shooting my calendar, and you get what you want, a little mattress time with a real-life hottie instead of a concrete fantasy." She put one finger on her cheek and pretended to ponder. "And didn't your assistant text you this afternoon about a job rescheduling?"

Patti had had Eden wriggling in her seat with her talk of all that hot, sweaty sex. It had been too long.

But she didn't want a soldier. That was just…she wasn't going there. "You're manipulating me."

"You're all black and white."

And Patti had just moved from manipulation to outright psychological warfare. She knew that was Eden's Achilles' heel. Eden would rather do something impulsive and stupid than be rigid and uncompromising like her father. Actually, it didn't take a psych degree to know that her upbringing probably drove her impulsive tendencies. "Remind me again why we're friends."

Patti remained unrepentant. "I tell you what—let's consult the cards. I'll do a reading for you."

"Fine. And if the cards say no, you won't mention the calendar job again." And Patti'd better not mention Eden being rigid like her father. Her father's unyielding mind-set had always been a point of contention.

Her BFF handed over the deck. "You know the deal. Shuffle. And if the cards say yes, you'll shoot my calendar. Ask the question and seal your destiny."

"Should I shoot the paratrooper calendar?" Eden carefully divvied the cards into three piles in a classic three-card spread—the past, the present and the outcome.

Patti took over from there. "The past," she intoned, turning over the top card. A shiver slid down Eden's spine and she could swear the breeze blew just a tad cooler for a second.

Then Patti spoke. "The King of Swords. An authority figure. The sword could indicate the military, which all fits with your father. And it is, after all, your dad's career that makes your past what it is."

"It fits," Eden said.

"Okay. Now, the present." Patti moved on to the second deck, and flipped over the card to reveal The Star card. Her wide smile revealed the slight gap in her front teeth. "You know the star portends a new beginning, a move to hope after a bad period. Maybe in your case a new way of seeing the military."

The hair on the back of Eden's neck stood up. Sometimes the message in the cards was vague but there certainly didn't seem to be any ambiguity here. Without saying anything she nodded for Patti to reveal the third card, the future.

One deft flick of her friend's wrist and they were both faced with The Knight of Swords.

"I'm screwed," Eden said.

"I guess it depends on your perspective." Patti grabbed the interpretation book that came with the cards and started flipping through it. "Let's make sure we get this absolutely right." She stopped. "Here we are. The Knight of Swords is bold and enthusiastic, but also imaginative and clever like his Queen. He's a great champion of good causes and inspires others by his idealism and dedication to any cause he adopts. He is decisive and, while others dither over a course of action, he will just plunge headlong into it, generally winning the day. He is a symbol of creative upheaval, usually leading to success." Patti smirked. "Yeah, if you were looking to turn the assignment down, you're definitely screwed."

"Okay. I'll shoot the calendar." It looked as if Eden would be spending a couple of days exactly where she didn't want to be—an Army base.

Tarot cards or no, however, she would not be having hot, sweaty sex with anyone. There was impulsiveness and then there was insanity. And she wasn't crazy yet.

LIEUTENANT COLONEL MITCH DUGAN, 82nd Airborne paratrooper, Special Forces, threw himself into the trench at a dead run. *Thwump*. He hit the hard ground and immediately began to wriggle on his belly beneath the razor-sharp barbed wire, as the bullets whizzed just above him. Faster. Lives depended on it. His and his men's. Failure was not an option.

He came to the end of the barbed-wire trench, maneuvered himself free and in one powerful motion pushed to his feet. Without pause, he sprinted in a zigzag pattern toward the sand-bag-rimmed bunker fifteen meters away. Putting on a final burst of speed, he finished the last five meters—shoulder rolling into the hole in the ground that provided his only protection. Thirty seconds later Captain Eli Murdoch dove into the hole, as well. Without a word, each man performed a quick, thorough visual scan of the surrounding area. Mitch nodded brusquely. Murdoch acknowledged it with his own nod.

"Alpha Company, clear," Murdoch, as detachment leader, reported the area safe. "Repeat, Alpha Company clear."

"Alpha Company, clear," the training instructor, Jenners, called back.

Mitch and Murdoch climbed out of the bunker, as did the rest of the twelve-man squad from the surrounding bunkers on the training ground. The "bullets" whizzing overhead had been simulated but Mitch never, ever, allowed himself to think of them as anything other than live fire and he'd cautioned the men to think the same. It kept them sharp, fast and careful.

Jenners approached Murdoch. "Damn fine job, Captain. Your squad set a new record today. If I'm ever in trouble, I know who I want sent in to haul my ass out of hot water."

Eli nodded. "We'll take care of you."

Mitch looked at the men who were just as dirty and sweaty as he was. As an evaluator, he'd challenged each of them to push harder, to set a new standard and rise to it. They had. Mitch had had his doubts about Staff Sergeant Tolbert, the team's Assistant Weapons NCO. Even though Tolbert had passed the rigorous training, Mitch wasn't sure the guy was willing to give the one hundred and ten percent required in a special forces unit. But even Tolbert had pulled out the stops. "Nice job. I'll see you all at 1300."

He waited until the men had cleared the training area to head toward the showers. Eli Murdoch walked with him. "Tolbert came through," Murdoch said, inadvertently echoing Mitch's earlier assessment.

"He's shaping up and falling in line."

Mitch had been totally unsurprised to find Murdoch assigned as a squad leader at Fort Bragg after he and Murdoch had earned their jump wings at Fort Benning back in June. Murdoch was the closest thing to a friend Mitch had ever allowed himself. They'd met six years earlier when they were both wet-behind-the-ears junior officers, fresh out of ROTC.

Murdoch and his wife, Tara, were good people. Mitch had even wound up buying a brick ranch-style home on the same street as Tara and Eli in the historic Haymount area of Fayetteville.

"By the way—" Oh, hell, he knew what was coming when Murdoch started out with *by the way.* "Tara wants to know if you'll join us for dinner on Saturday night."

Crossing the last of the dirt training field, Mitch cut to the chase. "Are any of her single friends going to be there?"

Murdoch shrugged and offered a smart-ass grin. "She didn't say."

"Your wife has more single friends than Louisiana has mosquitoes, and that's saying something." Unfortunately, Tara seemed hell-bent on introducing him to each and every one of them. Even Tara's homemade meat loaf and mashed potatoes wasn't worth another attempted hookup.

"I swear I didn't know Dizzy Donna was going to

be there last week." Murdoch threw his hands up in mock surrender. "*That* chick is a walking, talking nightmare."

Eli wouldn't get any argument from Mitch on that front. "Man, she's gotta stop worrying about my love life. And she might want to reconsider some of the crazies she calls friends."

"I know. I know. But it's a chick thing. Tara thinks you're great so you're the first person she thinks of when one of her girlfriends is looking for Mr. Right. If I didn't know she was crazy about me, it might piss me off." Murdoch offered an arrogant grin that said he wasn't remotely concerned about his wife's affections.

"Right." Murdoch and his wife, still newlyweds, were damn near embarrassingly in love. "Dizzy Donna. It fits." Mitch didn't require his dates to be Mensa candidates but all that woman could talk about was her favorite band.

Murdoch smirked. "She thinks you're *gay.*"

"What the fu—?" Mitch threw back his head and laughed. "She thinks I'm gay?"

"That's what she told Tara. She said she'd called you three times and you hadn't returned her calls. Therefore, you must be gay."

"I guess it didn't occur to her that I just wasn't interested. I thought if I ignored her, she'd get the message." He chuckled again. That was one way to get rid of her, he supposed. "Whatever. As long as she quits calling me. And it was more like three times a day."

"Ouch." Murdoch winced.

"Hey, I'm cool with letting her think I'm gay if it means she'll stop harassing me. She's definitely not my type."

Murdoch groaned. "Why'd you have to say that? Now Tara's going to want to know what your type is."

They walked into the gym building.

"Murdoch, how's she going to know about this part of our conversation if you don't tell her?" Mitch grinned. "Just keep your mouth shut." A tall order for Murdoch.

"In a perfect world, it would work that way, but Tara's got a way of…"

Actually, Mitch had seen Tara Murdoch in action. She did have a way. She'd make a helluva interrogator. "Fine. My idea of the perfect woman?" He thought about what constituted the ideal female. "Tall, thin, blond. Quiet. Athletic. Practical and organized. Someone who feels the same way I do about the military." Yep. That pretty much covered it.

They walked into the locker room. "Just for the record, while we're on the subject, do you ever just settle for maybe five out of eight on the requirement list?"

"What's the point of having a requirement list if you're going to settle?"

"Maybe compromise is a better word."

Mitch shrugged and pulled his T-shirt over his head. "Compromise. Settle. Same difference. And the answer is no. Why have standards if you don't stick to them?" He sat on the bench and began to unlace his boots.

How many times had his dad sworn he was going to keep a job this time, only to last a whopping two weeks? How many times had his mother vowed to stay sober only to fall off the wagon again? At twelve, thank God, he'd gone to live with his mother's parents and finally found some measure of sanity. His grandfather had retired from the Army and ran his household the way he'd run his career—organized, scheduled.

Mitch had learned early on that you either did what you said or you didn't. Good intentions didn't count for shit and actions did all the talking. That's what he embraced about the military—there was no room for the bullshit he'd grown up with. Life in the armed forces was cut and dried. Black and white. You knew exactly what was expected of you and you knew exactly where you stood. There was a rule and regulation for everything.

If not for going to live with his grandparents and pursuing his own military career, he might have followed in his parent's footsteps.

"So, you think you can make dinner Saturday night?"

Mitch pulled off the boots and followed with his sweaty socks. "Can't. I'm heading down to Charoux for a couple of days. The old man—" his grandpa liked being called that "—is turning eighty and I'm bringing in some of his Army buddies for his birthday. There aren't a whole hell of a lot of them left."

Mitch was looking forward to it. He only made the trip back home about once a year. Anything more and the old man accused him of "hovering" although Mitch always suspected his grandfather was determined not to be a burden. From the day Mitch had left Charoux, home had become whatever base he was stationed at for that moment in time.

"You flying?"

"Yeah." He stripped out of his pants. His briefs followed. "No time for a road trip." He enjoyed driving.

"I'll let Tara know."

Mitch snagged a towel and a bar of soap and headed toward the showers, leaving Murdoch in the locker room.

He turned on the water and stepped under the warm spray.

It'd be nice to take a break from the women Tara Murdoch kept throwing at him.

2

EDEN'S PALMS BEGAN TO SWEAT as she approached the wooden sign that proclaimed, "Fort Bragg, Home of the Airborne and Special Operations Forces." But then again, maybe it was just because she had to pee and not because she was entering the confines of Uncle Sam.

She'd flown in last night, picked up a rental car and checked into her hotel. She pulled up to the manned gate and waited behind three cars ahead of her for her base clearance. She'd been offered on-base lodging but had opted to shell out the money for a hotel room in civilian territory. She tapped her finger against the steering wheel, keeping time with the song on the radio. She was going to be late.

Time management wasn't her strong suit. She'd started out in what should have been plenty of time considering she was only fifteen minutes from the base. But she'd taken a wrong turn and wound up on some back road, then she'd passed the man selling late-season watermelons out of the bed of his pickup on the side of the road and the setting had such a quintessential Southern feel about it, she'd had to stop and chat with Junior Budgeton—that'd turned out to be his name. She'd taken a couple of photos and even a few candids when Junior's grandson had wandered down to the highway from a clapboard house squatting on a hill for one of his "Pap's treats"—a bright red slice of sticky, juicy watermelon with its green-rimmed rind. Bottom line—she was late.

Finally, she pulled up to the gate manned by a soldier wearing the signature maroon beret of the 82nd Airborne. He was polite but definitely not Hot Jumper calendar material. After checking his list and her ID he waved her through with instructions on how to get to where she was going.

Twenty minutes later—finding a parking spot had turned out to be far harder than finding the building itself—she hurried down the stretch of spotless military hallway as fast as her three-inch heels and pencil skirt allowed.

Being late, and was she ever, was considered heresy at Fort Bragg's Special Ops command center. Yet another aspect to love about the military—not. She was making the public relations, "thank you for having me here" call to the big office and then she'd meet with the public affairs people. She'd change afterward into jeans and flats.

Thirty whopping minutes on base and she already felt stifled. For the hundredth time, she lamented getting stuck with this Army Paratrooper calendar.

Damn Patti's black little soul to hell for rooking

Eden into this with limoncello and tarot cards. Her father would put it down to "artsy fartsy hyperbole" but she swore she could already feel the military's rigidity shutting down her brain.

Late, late, she's late for a very important date. As *The Alice in Wonderland* refrain echoed through her head, she chuckled to herself—after all, stressing wasn't going to turn back the clock—and put on a burst of speed as she turned the corner.

Thwump.

She collided with another moving force. She bounced straight off of a solid wall of soldier and her feet flew out from under her. Windmilling her arms uselessly, Eden landed on the polished gray-specked tile floor on her well-padded derriere. All the air whooshed out of her body.

Winded, she looked up past long legs, lean hips, a flat belly and a wall of chest, to a face that defined sinfully handsome. Chiseled lips, lean cheeks bisected by a sharp blade of a nose, and piercing eyes that were the most curious mix of gray and green, like cool, velvety moss on a stone statue.

A shock of recognition coursed through her quickly followed by a warm flush of desire. Mercury. He bore a striking resemblance to the statue in her garden except he wasn't naked and his wings were on a shoulder patch rather than on his feet. The thought that she'd like to see him naked chased through her head.

Sprawled at his feet ignominiously, quite suddenly

Eden felt light-headed as if her brain was oxygen deprived. That had to be why she continued to sit on her ass in the middle of the hallway and stare open-mouthed at the man who'd literally knocked her off her feet.

Lieutenant Colonel Mitch Dugan—she wasn't so flustered that she missed the silver oak leaf cluster on his shoulder or the name badge on his broad chest—leaned down, extending a helping hand.

Without considering it, she took it and suffered further indignity when it became apparent that her high heels and narrow tight skirt didn't lend themselves to being pulled to her feet. With a faint shake of his head he stated the obvious, "That's not working. Let's try this," he ordered. In a span of seconds, he released her hands, hooked his arms beneath her armpits and effortlessly stood her up.

For an instant she was against his hard body, his arms muscled bands around her, her breasts pressing against that unrelenting chest, her hips lined up with his, his chin—with a faint cleft, the photographer in her noted—at eye level. Flesh and blood. Yowza, he was hot. She tilted her head back to look at him and his enigmatic gray-green gaze snared hers.

A tremor jolted her from the soles of her feet to the top of her head. She was breast to chest with Mercury incarnate. He was a beautiful piece of flesh-and-blood man and Eden rolled with her impulse. It was a big base, after all. Who knew when she'd have this opportunity again?

She stood on her tip-toes, sliding another inch up Lieutenant Colonel Hardbody, and kissed him. A slow, deliberate press of her mouth against his lips. Firm, cool…magic.

As she pulled away, something indefinable flickered in his eyes. Laughter, whistles, and even a catcall erupted behind them. Oops. For a second she'd forgotten they weren't alone. A quick glance showed at least half a dozen men had witnessed that kiss. Definitely time for her to get to where she was going.

"Thanks, soldier," she said, stepping back and around where he stood like a stone statue. She headed down the hall.

"I'd suggest you avoid going around kissing *soldiers,*" he said. Ah, the Lieutenant Colonel was touchy about his rank. She stopped and pivoted to face him. "It could get you in trouble," he continued. His crisp voice carried a hint of Southern drawl that rendered it spine-tingling sexy. He paused and then tacked on, "Ma'am."

Tall, commanding, sure of himself—he had Special Ops written all over him. She'd made it a rule to never date, or sleep with, soldiers. She'd sworn there'd be no rolling around getting hot and sweaty while she was here. Hadn't she deemed that insanity? Especially since she was basically allergic to the military. It just seemed neater, cleaner to avoid any involvement with Uncle Sam's finest. But now there was *him.*

It was like the day she'd seen her house with its

walled garden and lemon tree and knew it was meant
for her. There was something about this Lieutenant
Colonel that made her want to slide beneath his seriousness and coax a smile from him.

She shot a flirtatious smile. "No worries. I only kiss
the ones who sweep me off my feet and then pick me
back up...soldier."

She turned on her heel and hurried down the hall. She
was now later than ever. She was also determined to find
out everything she could about one Lieutenant Colonel
Dugan.

One look into those gray-green eyes, one magic
kiss and she was fully, squarely in the camp of temporary insanity.

"LUCKY BASTARD," MCELHANEY said as Mitch joined
the platoon leaders waiting on the company commander to show up for the weekly briefing. He settled
into one of the brown metal folding chair in the briefing
room that resembled a high-tech classroom.

Even though Mitch wasn't a platoon leader, but was
stationed at Fort Bragg as a Special Ops training
evaluator, he participated in the weekly briefing as part
of his M.O. Each platoon leader headed six twelve-men
squads or detachments. It was Mitch's military occu-
pation to evaluate the training and readiness of the
company. As a strategic planner specializing in reconnaissance and evasion, Mitch trained alongside the detachments. In a perfect world, he would've preferred

to head a squad, but he'd been promoted too quickly and now held the evaluation position.

Special Forces soldiers underwent training in weapons, engineering and demolitions, communications, medicine, operations and intelligence. Each detachment had two noncommissioned officers who specialized in each field, however all were cross-trained and all were multilingual.

Mitch was well-versed in numerous Arabic and Middle Eastern dialects, which had stood him well on recon missions into both Afghanistan and Iraq. He'd also participated in and evaluated the Special Forces HALO training where jumpers pushed the limits—free-falling from a high altitude, which kept them off enemy radar, and opening their chutes within a thousand feet of the ground.

But the bottom line was most of the platoon leaders feared him. And there were a couple, McElhaney and Robertson, who downright disliked him because he'd found their squad training substandard. Mitch had no use for a commander who'd rather cover his own ass than make sure his men were as prepared as possible to go into a mission, do their job, and come out alive. There was no love lost between him and McElhaney. Robertson mostly gave him a wide berth.

"I know," Carter seconded McElhaney's comment. He looked at Mitch and shook his head, as if dumbfounded. "Dugan. Of all the guys to pick, she picks him."

"You damn well better believe that the next time I

see her coming, I'm going to knock her down and pick her back up," McElhaney said.

Ortiz, one of the five platoon leaders present, entered the conversation. "So who's your mystery woman, Dugan?"

Ortiz was a damn fine leader. His men carried an edge over the others. Mitch nodded. "Trouble," he said. "That's who she is."

Ortiz chuckled. "Does Trouble have a name?"

Trouble had a name alright. "Eden Walters." Eden. Depending on your perspective it could be the proverbial garden of paradise or the place where one found irresistible temptation. He was betting on the latter. The taste of her had been on his mouth the whole damn morning, the feel of the press of her breasts against his chest, the light flirty, floral scent had clung to his lapel…and those dancing midnight-blue eyes.

Unbidden, the image came to mind of Eden Walters sprawled sexily on her back, at his feet. She wasn't exactly pretty, her face was too angular, her features a bit too sharp, but she was arresting. He'd even go so far as to call her striking with her cap of short dark hair, creamy skin, and stunning blue eyes. And the woman had killer legs. Most definitely trouble. "Her old man's BMFIC at Campbell."

"No shit?" Carter looked suitably impressed. Being in charge of Fort Campbell, home to the only air assault division in the world, was a big deal.

"No shit. You're running your mouth about Brigadier General Max Walters's daughter."

McElhaney's grin was unrepentant and slightly unpleasant. "All I can tell you, buddy—" McElhaney definitely wasn't his buddy "—is he isn't here and she is. I bet I can get her to kiss me even without putting her on the floor."

Ortiz, married with two kids and a third on the way, shook his head.

Carter smirked. "Not if she sees me first, dickweed."

Mitch shook his head. What *had* she been thinking? She knew better. She'd grown up on military bases—she *had* to *know* better. Why not just wave a red flag in a field of bulls? The woman had to be crazy as hell.

And he should give a damn, why? Because he couldn't seem to move past her kiss. It wasn't as if he hadn't kissed and been kissed any number of times. But there'd been something about her kiss that seemed to linger against his mouth long after she was gone.

And quite frankly the idea of Carter or McElhaney or any of the other innumerable soldiers lining up for one of her kisses had him wanting to bang some heads.

"So, what's she doing here?" Ortiz asked. He was definitely the sharpest of the group, but Mitch had known that long before this discussion.

It had been easy intel to pick up. "She's a big-name photographer. She's putting together a calendar for a fundraiser."

"A calendar of what?" Carter said. "Like paratrooper of the month or something like that?"

"Something like that. The specific terms used were hardbody and hot."

"Guess that lets you off the hook, Dugan, since they're not looking for a hard-ass." McElhaney's smile held barely disguised dislike. "But she definitely needs to get a good look at me."

"Forget it," Carter jumped into the fray. "They'd need to put more than the back of your head on there and that's the only part of you that qualifies."

McElhaney's response was cut short when Company Commander Colonel Gus Hardwick—commonly known among the troops as Harddick—entered the room, strode to the table and chair in the front and started without preamble. Harddick wasn't one to squander words or time.

For over an hour they discussed maneuvers, upcoming missions, squad performance, individuals that needed help, testing for the week and general status updates.

Mitch could tell Hardwick was winding down by the inflection in his voice and all the material they'd already covered. That suited Mitch just fine. He had a boatload of pain-in-his-ass paperwork to review—that was the part of his job he loathed—before an afternoon training jump.

"We've got one more thing to cover. As you know by now, we have a visitor here in Alpha company." Harddick looked straight at him. "I'm sure we're all in agreement that any additional money going to supplement survivor benefits is a good thing." Hardwick paused. There wasn't a man in the room who wasn't remembering buddies lost in the line of duty and the families they'd left behind. And damn straight their widows and kids could use the extra dough. Just because there was a crazy, sexy woman in charge of the project didn't mean it wasn't worthwhile.

Hardwick continued, "The photographer wants to pick her own subjects rather than choose from a pool of volunteers. In fact, she'll be observing the training jump at Sicily this afternoon." McElhaney's platoon was scheduled for a HALO training jump in the Sicily Drop Zone at 1500 hours. Dugan, who'd be jumping with them, didn't miss McElhaney's smirk. The guy really was an asshole.

"If you or one of your men is approached, participation is strictly voluntary. However, remember it's in support of fallen comrades."

Mitch had a mental snapshot of Eden out at the barren Drop Zone in those ridiculous, impractical heels and tight skirt. For one crazy second he imagined the rush of the jump followed by the feel of her against him. That was it, that was what he hadn't been able to nail all morning. That instant, crazy rush when he was free-falling and then ripped the cord to open his chute—that was the same damn way he'd felt this morning when she'd kissed him in the hall. One single kiss from her and he'd had that ripped sensation. It was really kind of crazy. Mitch shifted in his seat. He didn't need to remember that kiss, the feel of her body against his, especially not now in the middle of a damn meeting.

"Keeping that in mind," Hardwick stared a hole into

Dugan, "I need a volunteer to oversee the logistics of the project, to escort Ms. Walters around the base and coordinate the schedules between training and the photo shoots."

Great. Mitch shook his head slightly.

"Ah, Dugan. I knew I could count on you."

Damn.

At the same time, McElhaney raised his hand. "I can handle that assignment, sir."

"Thanks, McElhaney, but Dugan beat you to it and you've got some training issues you need to address." Hardwick looked back to Mitch. "You seem to have a rapport with our visitor so I'm sure you'll handle this with your usual efficiency."

Volunteer his ass. This was obviously a we-expect-more-from-you-than-base-gossip reprimand. It sure as hell wasn't anything he would've truly volunteered for but it was obvious the woman needed a keeper. That much had been apparent when she'd kissed him in the hall. He was going to take a boatload of shit for this, but it was also sweet to knock McElhaney out of what he'd wanted. "Yes, sir."

"You'll report immediately to Public Affairs following this briefing. Consider yourself on-task."

"Yes, sir."

He'd had some ball-busting, gut-clenching assignments since he'd been in the Army and certainly since he'd earned his green beret. This, however, had all the makings of a clusterfuck.

3

EDEN SAT IN AN OFFICE SIMILAR to other military offices around the globe—she should know, she'd been in enough of them. Her nose twitched in recognition. There was a smell particular to a U.S. military installation, whether it was Hawaii or Germany or North Carolina.

"So, you want to locate the candidates yourself?" Sergeant Sanchez said, after glancing down at a file.

"That's right." It wasn't as if this was new information. Eden had reviewed the process on the phone with the Public Affairs liaison and then again when she'd met with them after her late courtesy call to battalion headquarters. Despite that conversation, they'd insisted they'd present her with calendar candidates. She'd been equally adamant she'd select her own. Because her way wasn't Army protocol, she'd been shifted to someone else. And then someone else again. Now, it was Sergeant Sanchez's turn to deal with her. Surely the third time was a charm—and they were burning daylight.

"Sergeant, I'm a professional photographer by

trade. I specialize in people—in knowing who and when to take a photo. It's what I'm trained to do."

Sanchez looked up from his paperwork, his brown eyes crinkling at the corners. "So, I don't tell you how to take a picture, and you don't tell me how to run my mission."

Yes! Finally, someone who understood something other than protocol. "That's pretty much it."

"How about we coordinate a schedule?"

It'd probably unnerve him if she broke into the Hallelujah chorus so she contented herself with saying, "You are a god among mere mortals."

On the other side of the green metal desk, Sanchez grinned. "I just need to fill out a couple of forms." He checked his watch. "And we had an escort lined up for you, a Captain Gibbens. Unfortunately, she went into early labor last night. We're waiting on her replacement."

Her hopes of getting this wrapped up in three days were becoming slimmer by the minute. She bit back a sigh and pasted on a smile.

"Oh. I hope everything turns out well with the baby." And with luck, they wouldn't send her another nine-month pregnant escort. Eden's neighbor had given birth last year and the woman hadn't been exactly full of energy in her eighth and ninth month. Eden couldn't imagine that Captain Gibbens had been looking forward to hunting down subjects and then working through photo shoots. Eden supposed it was too much to ask that they simply turn her loose unattended on base.

She noticed a framed snapshot of a dark-haired, dark-eyed toddler and a blond woman on Sergeant Sanchez's desk. "Your family?"

He nodded, practically beaming with pride. "My wife, Liz, and Cassie, my little monster. She just turned two."

"She looks just like you." While Sanchez's hair was close-cropped and the little girl boasted a head full of dark ringlets, her face was a mirror image of his.

"I know. Poor kid. She was born while I was on my last tour in Iraq."

"I'm sure you couldn't wait to get home to see her."

He grimaced. "I wanted to see her but I got sent home a little sooner than I expected." He lifted his left arm and for the first time Eden noticed a prosthetic hand. "Compliments of an insurgent IED, uh, that's improvised explosive device in civilian terms, also commonly known as a homemade bomb."

She knew exactly what an IED was and she hated it that he'd had firsthand experience with one. "I'm so sorry."

"Hey, I'm lucky. At least I made it home and I get to see my kid every day. I think this calendar…well, some of the guys in our unit who didn't make it home…they had kids, too." His eyes were somber. "Thank you."

She liked his spirit. Even in the face of having lost

a limb, he saw his cup as half full. She felt both humble and grateful in the face of his sacrifice on behalf of his country. She wanted to offer something in return, even though it didn't begin to compare. "I'm going to be here for a few days. If you'd like, I could photograph your family."

"For real?"

"For real."

"They're in New Mexico now—Liz's sister just had a baby—but they'll be back in a couple of days. Liz would be thrilled. Thank you."

"We'll do it maybe Thursday or Friday. I'll be free in the evenings."

She felt like an utter heel that she'd ever been resistant to shooting the calendar in the first place. This guy had lost a hand in service to his country and she'd whined about having to be on a military base for a handful of days? And now *he* was thanking *her.* "And you're very welcome."

The sergeant continued filling out one of the myriad forms but looked up with a grin, as if he was eager to move on to lighter conversation. "Spotted any calendar candidates yet?"

"I haven't really had a chance to scope things out. I've spent my entire morning being shuffled from one office to the next."

"That's the military for you—hurry up and wait."

Sanchez was friendly and outgoing. Now seemed the perfect time to inquire about the man who'd knocked her off her feet earlier. "Do you know a Lieutenant Colonel Dugan?"

"Yes, ma'am." A ready grin spread over his face. "I heard you met him earlier."

On base, gossip traveled faster than a speeding bullet. "We ran into one another." She answered his grin with one of her own.

"You've got guts. The Lieutenant Colonel can be sort of intimidating."

Dugan was hard, but not unkind. She'd seen enough of both kinds of people to recognize the difference.

"Is he married?" She shifted back in her chair and brushed a speck off of her skirt, her heart thumping like mad in her chest. She hadn't noticed a ring but lots of married guys didn't wear them—especially guys who went through combat training where a ring could prove to be a hazard.

Sanchez grinned. He so had her number. "Not married. I don't know about a girlfriend though."

Relief rolled through her and she realized just how tense she'd been, waiting on his answer. "At least I won't have an angry wife looking me up."

"That's always a plus. My wife would go ballistic." He shook his head as if it was a scary thought but the affection in his voice spoke volumes. "And I take it you're not married?"

"No. No husband at home." Ha. She couldn't even find a guy she wanted to date on a regular basis. Unlike a lot of the women she knew, she wasn't husband hunting. She liked her house, her job and her own company. And most of all, she liked her independence.

"There are lots of guys who'll be glad to—"

A sharp rap on the door interrupted Sanchez.

In one of those real-life-was-stranger-than-fiction moments, Lieutenant Colonel Dugan himself entered the office.

SERGEANT SANCHEZ SHOT TO HIS FEET. "Can I help you, sir?"

Dugan waved him back down. "As you were, Sergeant. I'm here to pick up Ms. Walters." Mitch continued to maintain eye contact with the soldier behind the desk but every other part of him was fully tuned into the woman in the room. He heard her sharp intake of breath at his announcement.

His body tightened in a totally involuntary response to her scent, the memory of that quick, but oh-so-sensual, slide of her curves against him, the taste of her kiss. "I'm Ms. Walters's escort for this project."

He glanced at her, judging her reaction. Her amazing midnight-blue eyes widened with surprise and a flicker of something indefinable. There was something in the way she'd looked at him when she lay sprawled at his feet, a slight recognition, a touch of familiarity. Mitch, however, was sure he'd never met her before. Given the way he responded to her, he'd have definitely remembered. She wasn't a woman a man easily forgot.

"*You're* Captain Gibbens replacement?" Sanchez said.

The disbelief in the sergeant's voice didn't surprise Mitch. This certainly wasn't Mitch's typical assignment but then again, Hardwick was making an example of Mitch and having a little sadistic fun at Mitch's expense. Hardwick was that kind of fun-loving guy.

Mitch offered a short laugh, mocking himself. "Do you think I can't handle the assignment, Sergeant?"

For a split second Sanchez looked as if he couldn't decide whether to laugh along with him or not. Sanchez opted for the not. "No, sir," he said. "I'm one-hundred percent sure you can handle any assignment, sir."

Sitting in the chair to Dugan's left, Eden Walters made a choking sound.

Mitch turned to her and felt a tightening inside him. "Are you okay, Ms. Walters?"

She had a way of smiling with her eyes. It was like the sun coming out. He'd noticed it this morning in the hallway. "I'm fine." She brushed her fingers against her throat and he found himself fascinated by the pale column of flesh. Would it taste the same as her mouth? Would her pulse throb against his tongue if he licked just the right spot? "Just something stuck for a moment."

Right. Like maybe a laugh.

"Okay. Paperwork completed," Sanchez said. "You've

got a guide. You're on your way." Sanchez rounded the desk and nodded.

Eden rose to her feet and Mitch automatically glanced down at her red heels and the shapely curve of her calf. Those shoes were going to have to go before they went out to Sicily, today's jump site. They were sexy as hell, but totally impractical. And every guy there would be thinking about stripping her down to nothing but those heels…well, and maybe a pair of panties. That's sure as hell what he was thinking about right now and he was damn certain every other man at Sicily would be doing the same. The heels had to go.

"Thank you…for everything," she said, giving Sanchez a quick hug and a smile. "You've got my number. Call me when you want to get together. I'm serious."

"I'm going to take you up on that."

"Good. I'm really looking forward to it."

She was friendly, Mitch would give her that. She'd kissed him a couple of hours ago and now Sanchez was her new best friend.

Mitch held the office door for her. Fixing her over-size purse more firmly on her shoulder, she brushed past him into the hallway. Her perfume teased his nostrils with its light, flirty aroma. The image of her in those heels, her arms twined around him, that scent surrounding him suddenly flashed through his mind.

He determinedly dragged his thoughts elsewhere.

What was it about this particular woman that slid in beneath his radar? It didn't matter, he just better get the hell over it—walking down the hall with a hard-on struck him as a piss-poor idea.

Was she setting up a "get together" with Sanchez now, even though the guy was married? It was absolutely, totally none of his business...except for the fact that she was his mission for the next few days.

"Sanchez has a wife," he said, as they walked down the hall.

For a stretch of thirty seconds or so, the only sound between them was the *tap-tap-tap* of those ridiculously high heels of hers against the tile floor. And then she laughed—a rich, full vibration of genuine mirth. "You thought...I *know* he's married. We discussed his wife and daughter. He was so nice and helpful I offered to shoot his family when they get back in town. Shoot as in photograph."

"Right. Just making sure." Dammit, for the second time in less than six hours she had thrown him for a loop, and he didn't do loops. He moved on to the day's events. "You're scheduled to observe a training jump at 1500 hours today." Fantasies would be flying and especially after the conversation between McElhaney and Carter. The thought of watching her choose other men didn't sit well with Mitch. "You need to change your shoes."

She arched an amused brow in his direction. He was glad she found him entertaining. "I have shoes."

"I'm aware of that, but they're not practical."

Her nose tilted up slightly at the end with the faintest sprinkling of freckles across the bridge. "Lieutenant Colonel, I have a pair of flats in my car, along with a pair of slacks. I know I can't go to a jump dressed like this. Despite the impression I might've given you earlier, I'm not a total idiot."

Regardless of the fact that they were in the Public Affairs building, and that a small knot of soldiers stood at one end of the hall chatting, that kiss loomed suddenly between them, binding them as firmly as the silk cords on a parachute. Her gaze dropped to his mouth and she moistened her plump lower lip with the tip of her tongue. Heat charged through him and for a second his only thought was to pull her to him and thoroughly explore her mouth. And then sanity returned, yanking him back on-task. He was never off-task. "Idiot wasn't exactly the term that came to mind, Ms. Walters."

He held the door and she preceded him out into the parking lot and the warm, October sun. "If you say so." She nodded her thanks as he held the door for her, then shot him an infectious smile he found himself wanting to return. "Give me a few minutes to change and I'll be ready. I'm quick."

Once again, same as this morning, he watched her walk, the sway of her hips capturing his attention. Deliberately he looked away. The last thing he wanted or needed was to be caught ogling Brigadier General Max

Walters's daughter's ass in the parking lot—even though it was ogle-worthy.

He checked out the horizon. Clear skies, moderate wind in from the northeast. It'd be a nice day for the training jump.

Only someone who'd ever jumped understood the rush of adrenaline, that roar of the wind as your body hurtled toward the ground and then the yank and glide as your parachute unfurled and you rode the air currents once more back to terra firma. Unfortunately, his ass was grounded this time around by a woman with an infectious smile, midnight-blue eyes and a helluva kiss.

EDEN SAT IN THE PASSENGER SEAT of Lieutenant Colonel Dugan's immaculately restored red-and-white Ford Bronco.

"What year is this?" she asked, rubbing her hand over the seat.

"Sixty-nine," he said.

She swallowed hard and redirected her mind from the very sexual place it had just jumped to and back to his truck. "Very nice."

"Thanks. It was a two-year project. Just a hobby of mine."

She suspected nothing was "just" with him. He struck her as very focused, very intense. "When you're not deployed?"

"Right."

Eden knew better than to ask where he'd been, what he'd done. She'd been nine years old when her father had been in the First Gulf War. When he'd come home, it had never been talked about. What happened on a deployment wasn't up for conversation in the Walters household. Training, however, frequently popped up.

"So, how hard will it be to show up and not jump today?"

After an initial moment of surprise, he laughed. "It's pretty dam—I mean darn hard."

His changing the damn to darn struck her as sweet. And she'd bet Lieutenant Colonel Special Ops Hard-ass would just love to be thought of as sweet. She smiled at the thought.

"It's okay. I've heard curse words before."

"I guess I better work on my poker face," he said, with an unexpected self-deprecating sense of humor.

"Not necessarily." She shrugged. It wasn't his expression. It was more as if she were picking up vibes from him, which would just sound beyond strange if she shared that. Instead, she reasoned, "Most jumpers love to jump."

"Have you ever done it?"

She absolutely couldn't stop thinking about sex around him. She knew good and well he was asking if she'd ever parachuted, but all she could think about when he said *done it* was, well, doing it. She'd been in some jacked up hormonal state ever since she'd found herself at his feet this morning.

The close confines of his truck didn't help, either. She was *achingly* aware of everything about him. He smelled good—a mixture of faint aftershave, uniform starch and yummy man. She'd grown up around men in uniform and they'd never done a thing for her. But Mitch Dugan was smokin' hot in his…and she'd bet he was even hotter out of it.

"How can you know you won't like it if you've never tried it?" The timbre of his voice rippled over her.

In a flash she was imagining the two of them, naked in her courtyard, surrounded by the sultry New Orleans heat and the inky dark night. The brush of his skin against hers, his breath warm against her neck, his arm wrapped around her waist, pulling her tighter against him….

She drew a slightly unsteady breath. "I'm open to trying lots of things—" *If he only knew.* "But some experiences are better left untried. The only way I'm jumping out of a plane is if someone throws me out the door."

"Then it's probably better that you don't get on a jump plane. It's been known to happen." His grin held a wicked edge. "And here I'd pegged you to be the daring type, Ms. Walters." There was no mistaking his challenge. The air between them felt fraught with sexual energy. When was the last time she'd felt so engaged by someone?

"Really? Does a woman have to be daring to kiss you, Lieutenant Colonel?"

The look he shot her set her nipples tingling.

Sweet mercy. "I was talking about the red heels. They send a message."

"Really? Is that your specialty? Decoding intelligence?"

"Red heels don't require a specialization."

"So, exactly what message do you *think* they send, Lieutenant Colonel?"

He made an efficient left turn. "They say 'I'm bold. I'm not like everyone else here.' And that kiss, that was all about telling everyone they might do what they're told, but you'll do what you want to do."

"Maybe you're partially right."

"I'm always right."

"Not this time, soldier. Do you ever do something just because the impulse strikes you?"

"No." Unequivocal.

No surprise there. Her question had mostly been rhetorical. Lieutenant colonels, especially one his age, were not men of impulse.

She shifted in her seat, turning toward him. "That kiss was pure impulse. The only message there was I wanted to kiss you, so I did." She did feel a tad remorseful although she couldn't bring herself to regret it. "I know that's why you wound up assigned to this. You no more volunteered for this assignment than I did." He slanted her a quick glance. "Colonel Hardwick's warped sense of humor is almost legendary. I've heard my dad talk about him more than once. He obviously thought you needed slapping down for being indiscreet." She shook her head. "Trust me, I'm fairly familiar with soldiers and how they think."

"I guess that happens when your father is a Brigadier General."

Was he reminding himself or her? "This is what happens when your father is a Brigadier General—I'll get a phone call tonight from my mother and in the conversation she'll manage to work in my father's disappointment in my behavior. It's yet another reason I avoid Army bases," she said, looking out the window. A group of soldiers stood at attention on a bare expanse of ground, obviously some review or another. They were all alike. There was no room for any individuality. Everything here was all the same Army-issue green or tan. She suppressed a faint shudder and looked back at Dugan. "It's like living in a glass house and every action and reaction reflects back on my father. Believe me, I know." She'd been reminded often enough in the past. Damn straight she knew now. Reminders weren't necessary. "Growing up, our household was run with military precision and structure."

"It beats the hell out of the alternate. Without structure you have chaos. No one thrives in chaos."

He hadn't glanced at her but there was a slight change in his tone, his inflection that said more than the mere words. Authenticity. Authority. That's what it was. His tone bespoke firsthand knowledge.

"Something in between would be nice." He merely quirked an eyebrow at that. The sun slanted through the windshield, etching his profile against the backdrop of blue sky outside his window. Gooseflesh prickled her. Good Lord but he was beautiful. She could look at the sharp slant of his nose, the slope of his forehead, the cut of his cheekbones, and the clean-shaven jaw that gave way to that faintly clefted chin all day long. "It doesn't have to be one or the other."

"Things are almost never fifty-fifty. They usually tend to sway one direction or the other. I'll take structure and precision any day."

Why did she have this sick feeling in the pit of her stomach, as if she'd been handed a treat and then told she couldn't have it? "Obviously," she said in a crisp tone, "or the Army would be an impossible career choice for you. But it's not for everyone. Take this morning, for example. Public Affairs wanted to give me a list of calendar candidates."

His look clearly questioned why that was a problem. "It does seem more efficient considering the size of this base."

"But it's not efficient if they're not the right candidates. That's part of *my* specialization. I've got an eye for people. And that's the reason I'm here. See, a little flexibility would've actually made this morning much more efficient."

"What makes one candidate better than another? Don't you just need twelve well-built, easy-on-the-eyes guys?"

"It's not that straightforward. There's something, and

I don't know exactly how to describe it, that sets people apart in a photo. You would be perfect to photograph."

"Forget—" He stopped himself. "I'm certain you'll find twelve much better candidates than me."

She laughed. "Relax, soldier. You're not calendar material." The idea of Dugan posing for the camera instinctively struck her as all wrong.

That elicited a surprised laugh. "I'm not sure whether I'm relieved or insulted."

"That came out wrong." She tilted her head, studying him. "Of course you've got the face and build—" Her gaze skimmed his trim but muscular frame. "And there's an intensity about you that would photograph well." She was thinking aloud, trying to understand her reticence. While he did have all the components for a good candidate, every part of her protested putting his photo on display for everyone to see. "But not for this project."

Technically, putting Dugan in the calendar shouldn't be any different than including any of the other hard-bodied jumpers, men that women would be willing to part with fourteen dollars and ninety-seven cents plus tax to ogle to their heart's content. But it was different. *He* was different.

He was private project material.

4

MITCH WATCHED THE LAST OF the jumpers glide through the sky. It was the first time he'd had to stand idly by and watch a training jump—the high-altitude, low-opening HALO that he liked so much, at that—since he'd earned his wings. It sucked. Once you knew that feeling, that exhilaration of free-falling through the sky, the adrenaline kick that came with the chute engaging, it was hard to stand by and not participate.

Not, however, as hard as it might have been under other circumstances. Eden Walters intrigued him. Despite their interesting conversation on the drive out to the jump field, she'd been all business in assessing potential subjects once they'd arrived. So far she'd pegged three guys that fit her criteria. Mitch had been observing her, intrigued in spite of himself when she'd get that particular "ah-hah" look on her expressive face, the signal that she'd spotted someone who clicked for her.

"Okay, what about him? Who is he?" she asked nodding toward the last five guys on the field gathering their chutes.

"The guy with the dark hair?" Her other three choices had dark hair.

"No. The blond."

Sonofabitch. Of all the soldiers at Fort Bragg, McElhaney sure as hell didn't deserve to represent paratroopers in a calendar. Nonetheless he gave her his name, rank and platoon contact information.

She jotted it down on her notepad.

McElhaney was a terrible choice. Mitch's gut told him the guy was bad news. Although his squad was never in danger of failing, they were certainly the worst prepared. As a leader, McElhaney left a lot to be desired. Hell, from what he'd seen of the guy so far, McElhaney left a lot to be desired even as a human being.

"He's not a good candidate." Mitch hadn't commented on any of the others, but Eden needed to know McElhaney would be a problem.

Eden paused. "How's that?" She turned her gaze on him and for a moment he was snared in the dark blue of her eyes. Damn it all to hell, he felt as if his stomach actually somersaulted. He'd faced down armed enemy combatants and not felt so off-balanced.

"You'll find him difficult to work with."

A frown creased her forehead. Funny how that only made her look sexier. "In what way?"

"For starters, he doesn't like me worth a damn because I called him on some substandard training. And since I'm part of this project now…" He shrugged.

Her frown deepened. "I just need to photograph him for the calendar. So far he's the only blond I've found."

"He's going to hit on you." Mitch got to the real point.

Her frown disappeared and she shrugged. "What? Does he make a pass at anything in a skirt?" She shook her head with a look that said *typical guy.*

Anything in a skirt? Did she not have a clue just how damn hot she was? "Let's just say he's got a point to prove. He was already planning to make a play for you."

She nodded, wrinkling her nose. "Thanks for the heads-up."

That was it? He was used to giving orders and having them followed. "You should strike him from your list."

Dammit, difficult, contrary woman that she was, she laughed at his directive. "I'm a big girl, Lieutenant Colonel. Believe it or not, I've had men make passes at me before."

He could believe it. All day. Even now, in the middle of the afternoon, in the middle of a damn jump zone, her gorgeous mouth had him tied up in knots. The thought of McElhaney making a play for her had him seeing red. What was up with that?

"I can handle it," she continued. "After all, I've got to be professional about this. I need a blond and he's got the looks and the build. Thank you, though."

"Sure." She hadn't exactly been professional when

she'd kissed him this morning, but whatever. If he was honest about it, that's what had his back up—McElhaney *would* make a play for her.

The cocky bastard's overly large ego would be inflated when she picked him out as a potential calendar candidate. That would only make him more determined to show everyone he could seduce the woman who'd kissed Dugan right out from under his nose.

As if their conversation had summoned the sneaky son of a bitch, McElhaney strolled over.

"Hi, I'm Captain Don McElhaney," he said, offering his hand to Eden, patently ignoring Mitch.

She offered McElhaney her hand and that same open, sunny smile she'd had for Sanchez. Mitch gritted his teeth. "Eden Walters. I was just telling Lieutenant Colonel Dugan I thought you'd make an excellent calendar subject."

Dugan wanted to smack the smugness right off of McElhaney's face. "I'm flattered. What month were you thinking?"

She retrieved her hand from McElhaney's grasp and laughed. "I was thinking April or May. One of the spring months. Do you have a preference?"

"July. It's always…hot."

Honest to God, McElhaney was an asshole of the highest order.

"It might work. I'll pencil you in for July and we'll

see." Was her smile just a tad more distant as she wrote in her notebook?

"How about dinner? We could talk about the calendar shoot…and things people can do in hot months."

Mitch clamped his jaw down to keep from telling McElhaney what he could do to himself in any month. It shouldn't matter who Eden went to dinner with. Hell, he'd only just met her. But, insanely, unreasonably it did. And since he didn't trust McElhaney as far as he could throw him, it mattered even more.

"Sorry." She shook her head. "I've got other plans."

"You could always change those plans," McElhaney said, pressing the matter.

For just a second, she glanced in Mitch's direction. It was enough.

"No, she can't," Mitch said, verbally stepping into the fray.

McElhaney's arrogant smile remained but his eyes hardened at Mitch's intervention and the implication that Mitch was part of her plans. "You're going to miss your ride, McElhaney." Mitch nodded toward the transport buses waiting to haul the soldiers and gear back to the hangar.

"Thanks for the heads-up, Dugan."

"Don't mention it."

"I'm looking forward to working with you on this," McElhaney said to Eden. He reached into his pocket and pulled out a piece of paper, passing it to her. "Give me a call if you want some company."

McElhaney had obviously planned to approach her all along. Mitch didn't know anyone who went on a jump carrying their name and phone number in their pocket.

"Well, that was interesting. I thought I might pass out from the amount of testosterone zinging around me," she said dryly. "You pegged him dead on."

"And he's still on your list?"

"Of course. I need a blond and those intense blue eyes of his should pop in a photograph. I don't have to like him to shoot him."

"I usually don't like the people I shoot," he said in a moment of dark humor, relieved to hear she hadn't actually liked McElhaney. That meant she'd be on her guard with him. She *needed* to be on her guard with him.

She wrinkled her nose at Mitch and tucked her notebook into her purse. "So, where are we going for dinner, Lieutenant Colonel?" she asked, her look bold, direct, flirting, challenging.

Dinner wasn't required of him. They both knew that. Dinner was a bad idea. Kissing her again was an even worse idea, yet he had a feeling that dinner would lead to just that. She was the daughter of a brigadier general. She was trouble. Trouble he didn't need.

He opened his mouth fully intending to say no. That was the plan. To politely turn her down.

"What are you hungry for?"

Dammit. That was not what he meant to say. Instinctively he glanced at her mouth and then to her dark blue eyes. What he saw in her gaze confirmed what he knew in his gut.

She might be trouble he didn't need, but she was trouble he *wanted*.

AN HOUR LATER DUGAN PULLED HIS red-and-white Bronco into the empty parking spot next to her rental. She'd accomplished much more than she'd thought she would, given the fact that half her morning had been spent being shuffled from office to office. Actually, she and Dugan made a very efficient team. She'd found half a dozen soldiers for the project, as well as four potential shot locations.

"How about I pick you up at your hotel at 1930 hours?"

"I'll be ready."

"It's very casual," he said. Eden had requested a nearby restaurant. First and foremost, she liked to think she was contributing to the local economy when she frequented neighborhood eateries, especially considering independent restaurant owners were showing big courage given the failure rate. Second, she liked to sample the local flavor of wherever she was.

"I can do casual," she said. She couldn't imagine why he'd think otherwise unless he was seeing her as the daughter of a brigadier general rather than the person she was.

"And the food can be a little messy, but you'll never taste better ribs."

The look in his eyes set off a fluttering low in her belly. All she could think was hot, messy sex. And judging from that flash of a glimmer in his eyes, it had occurred to him, as well. The idea seemed to dance between them and she wet her bottom lip with the tip of her tongue. "I can definitely do messy."

His gaze tangled with hers and Eden found it suddenly very difficult to breathe.

His jaw tightened, he nodded and the moment was gone…but it had been there. It had been there in spades. "I'll see you then."

Eden climbed out, and he waited until she'd started her car and backed out behind her. Ten minutes later she was off base and he'd turned toward his office to cover some paperwork.

Fifteen minutes after that, she was in her hotel room. Her hands not quite steady, she hit Patti's speed-dial number.

Patti answered on the second ring. "What's up?"

"You might want to sit down."

"Oh, boy. This is going to be good."

"I don't know about good, but it's got to be fast."

"Talk, girl. Talk."

Eden talked. She filled Patti in on the day, leaving nothing out. "And now we're going to dinner." And she knew with all the tension stretching between them, the awareness, the dampness between her thighs, it wouldn't just be dinner. The idea both excited her and terrified her. "Patti, he's so not the man I'm looking for. He's in the wrong profession. And he's intense. He loves all the things about the Army that make me crazy, but sweet mercy…there's something about him."

"Have you lost your mind?"

That was the entire point of the phone call. She thought she had. "I think so. But he's so, well, beautiful, that when I kissed him this morning…"

"No, you moron, I mean why are you even questioning what you should do? Go for it."

"What?"

"Go for it. You've only got a few days. Think of it as the ultimate affair. You get to do Mercury in the flesh. Where's the downside to that?"

A three-day affair with Lieutenant Colonel Mitch Dugan… The idea slid over her with a deliciousness that left her tingling, aroused, wanting. "I don't know. I just know I feel as if I've fallen into a river and I'm being swept along by a fast-moving current. This isn't what I wanted…isn't what I was looking for."

She paced to the hotel window and stared out at the sea of lights that was Fayetteville and Fort Bragg.

"What were you looking for then?"

Resting her forehead against the cool glass pane, Eden closed her eyes, trying to sort out her uncertainty, the turmoil inside her. "This is just so intense." Just like Mitch.

"So give yourself three days of intense sexual

pleasure. Heck, considering that you only have three or four days there, intense is a good thing."

Patti didn't understand. It was insane to ache for a man she'd just met, to long for a virtual stranger's touch. "So you don't think I'm crazy?"

"Crazy is sitting around fantasizing about some stone statue in your courtyard and then passing up on the real deal."

Something clicked into place for Eden. How many signs did she need? Wasn't she the queen of impulse? Hadn't she been the one who'd kissed Mitch this morning in the first place? Then why the cold feet? She pushed aside the thought that maybe it was because Mitch Dugan was different from any other man she'd ever met.

"I guess it would be quick in and quick out, wouldn't it?"

"I hope for your sake, it's not too quick."

The very thought made her quiver. "Very funny."

"It was, wasn't it?"

A thought occurred to Eden and she laughed aloud, knowing her voice held a hint of hysteria.

"What?" Patti asked.

"We're sitting here talking about quick ins and outs and he still calls me Ms. Walters."

On the other end, Patti chuckled. "Yeah, you might want to move to a first-name basis sooner than later."

She glanced at the digital clock beside the bed. She better hustle if she was going to shower and change before they went out to dinner. "Hey, I've got to go."

"Okay. Give me a call when you have time. I'll need an update."

Ha. What Patti really meant was that she'd want details. "I'll call…and thanks."

She tossed the phone to the bed and stripped, her body already tensing, anticipating Mitch's touch.

5

"HOW WAS ROUND ONE OF photographer sitting?" Murdoch asked with a grin, propping his shoulder against Mitch's doorjamb.

"Wait one sec," Mitch said. He finished the last of the reports, added it to the stack and leaned back in his chair, crossing his hands behind his head. "It was… interesting."

Murdoch dropped into the chair opposite Mitch. "No shit?"

"Actually, yeah."

"If she gets a look at me, she'll want me on her list for sure," Murdoch said with a grin.

"Arrogant bastard."

"Hey, have *you* made her list?"

Mitch wasn't about to relay that particular conversation to his friend. "You know, come to think of it…she seems to be looking for arrogant bastards, so you might stand a chance. She picked McElhaney."

Murdoch muttered a profanity that insulted both McElhaney and McElhaney's mother.

"I know. I tried to give her the heads-up."

"I wish you had something to nail him with," Murdoch said.

Mitch shrugged. "He's doing that himself. He's sloppy. It's going to catch up with him, sooner or later."

"The sooner the better. Are you heading out to Louisiana Friday night or Saturday morning?"

"I'm trying for Friday night. The old man's get-together is on Saturday night, so I'll get back sometime Sunday." Mitch grinned, as excited about reuniting the former soldiers as he'd been about anything in a long time. "It's going to be a damn good time. I'm glad I told him about it. He's been looking forward to it for months now."

"How many are coming?"

"Five. It was originally seven, but two guys died in the last six months."

"That's what happens when you're dealing with old dudes."

"Yep. So I'm checking the old man out and taking him to the VFW for the party."

"Reliving the glory days."

"That's what old soldiers do." Mitch grinned. "We'll be just like them one day. Talking about *remember when we went through jump training...that mission into northern Iraq.*"

"It's cool that you've pulled this together for them."

"I used to go to his battalion reunions with him when I was a kid. The guys told the same stories over and over, but I never got tired of listening to them. And now there's just a handful of his buddies left. I think I'm looking forward to seeing the old geezers as much as he is." Mitch glanced at the clock on the wall. "Hey, I've got to get out of here."

"So you *are* going to dinner with Eden Walters. Tolliver told his wife—" Mitch remembered Tolliver being in the last group of five jumpers. He must've overheard the conversation between McElhaney, Mitch, and Eden. "Who in turn told my wife who promptly called me to tell me I was holding information out on her," Murdoch continued. "So, where are you taking her?"

"She wanted something local so we're going to—"

"Wait," Murdoch interrupted, throwing up a cautionary hand. "Don't tell me unless you want us to show up. Because if you tell me, you know Tara's going to want to check her out."

Mitch came close to telling Murdoch anyway. It'd certainly keep dinner from getting too intimate if Tara and Murdoch showed up. His better judgment told him to give Murdoch the name of the restaurant. But was that what he really wanted?

Mitch's entire body tightened when he remembered her scent, the brief feel of her body against his, the fleeting taste of her mouth…and the look in her dark blue eyes when she'd all but dared him to take her to dinner.

Apparently, his better judgment had skipped town when it came to Eden Walters. He found himself shaking his head. "Just tell her you couldn't pry it out of me."

"She's going to kill me."

"Yeah, but I think you enjoy it, Murdoch."

Murdoch sobered. "Look man, you might want to proceed with caution considering her old man's a brigadier general."

"We're only going out to dinner."

"She kissed you this morning. It's already all over the base. And you know as well as I do that facts get distorted with every retelling."

Mitch suspected Brigadier General Max Walters was fully aware of what his daughter was like. Otherwise he was pretty damn sure he'd have already been called on the carpet about it. "Okay. I hear you."

He had just enough time to shower, shave and put on fresh civvies before he headed her way.

And it was kind of alarming just how much he was looking forward to doing just that.

EDEN'S HEART RACED AS MITCH Dugan pulled up in front of her hotel. She walked out to meet him and paused as he opened the passenger door of his truck for her. "I hope you weren't waiting too long, Ms. Walters."

She brushed past him to slide inside the Bronco. She didn't actually touch him but she was unbearably aware of his nearness. He'd showered. She could smell the fresh mix of soap, shampoo, clean clothes and man. His body heat drew her like a warm fire on a cold night. The errant thought that she'd been waiting on him a lifetime chased through her head. It was as disconcerting as the man himself. "No. I wasn't waiting long at all. You're right on time Lieutenant Colonel...but then I knew you would be."

He paused in closing the passenger door, a gleam of humor in his moss-green eyes. "Predictable?"

"Just military," she said, reaching for her seat belt. He closed the door without comment and rounded the truck to climb in the driver's seat.

Eden plowed ahead as he pulled out of the parking lot. "Now's probably a good time to tell you, you should just call me Eden. Ms. Walters has me looking over my shoulder for my mother."

He offered an abrupt nod. Well, not exactly abrupt. Economical. Everything about Mitch Dugan was together and efficient...well, except for when she'd kissed him this morning. "Roger that, Eden." Wow. That sent a little shiver through her and notched up her temperature a couple of degrees. His underlying Southern drawl was a little more pronounced when he said her name and it rolled off his tongue like a sweet whisper of seduction. "Lieutenant Colonel Dugan's a mouthful," he said without cracking a smile. "Why don't you just call me Lieutenant Colonel?"

Talk about hard core...she was pretty sure her mouth gaped a bit and he grinned at her. "That was a joke. My name is Mitch." His grin weakened her knees.

She laughed. He'd had her from the moment she'd fallen at his feet, but throw in a sense of humor and she was an utter goner. "You got me with that."

A slow smile, steeped in sensuality, tugged at his lips, thickening the air between them. Three days. She had three days with this man and she knew simply falling into bed with him wouldn't work for her. Some women could do stranger sex, one-night hookups—sometimes she envied them that ability, but it wasn't in her makeup. While she could do a brief fling, she had to at least know more about him than his name and his rank.

"So, Mitch." Simply saying his name sent a little thrill coursing through her. "Why the military?"

"My grandfather was career Army. An NCO." She noted that while his grandfather had been a noncommissioned officer, an enlisted man, Mitch was not only an officer, but a high-ranking one at a very young age. Interesting. "I grew up on his stories. I just knew it was where I belonged and what I was supposed to do, to be. I can't think of any greater honor than serving my country. And I like the structure, the order."

His hands on the steering wheel caught her attention. They were capable, masculine hands—well-shaped in that they weren't too narrow nor too square, his fingers blunt-tipped, his wrists carrying a smattering of dark hair. She remembered the feel, the tingle of his hands against her back when he'd hauled her to her feet this morning.

Her belly fluttered at the memory. And her people instincts zeroed in on what he'd not said as much as what he had. "What about your parents?"

"We're not close. I didn't have much structure growing up. I almost failed third grade because I was absent so much. They couldn't bother to get up in the morning and if they didn't care, I didn't care. I stayed up half the night playing video games."

He clamped his mouth shut and she knew he'd said way more than he'd ever intended. Now that particular topic was closed.

"What about you?" he asked. "Why photography?"

She was good at reading people and his question rang with genuine curiosity, although she could tell he was still quite happy to change the subject. "We moved all over the world and if you've seen one base, you've seen most all of them. And then, when we were living in Hawaii, on the big island, my aunt sent me a camera for Christmas. There was something about looking through that camera lens. Just a sense of 'this is me.' Does that sound crazy?"

"Nope. Not a bit. That was exactly the way the military was for me. Do you mainly photograph people?"

"Not just people. More like people in their element, when the backdrop tells their story, along with their face and their expression."

"How do you know when you find that?"

"It's an instinct. Photographer's intuition. Sometimes you just know when something's right. When it fits or clicks into place—even if you don't want it to be right."

He stopped at a red light and turned toward her. He had a way of looking at her that left her feeling as if he was peering into her very soul. She connected with people all the time, but this was different. It was as if he had access to the very core of her being, which was crazy since she'd only just met him. Still, it was very real, nonetheless.

"Is your instinct ever wrong?" he asked.

"I can't say it's ever failed me. It's only when I'm stubborn and ignore it because it's not what I want to hear that I wind up in trouble."

"Does that happen often?" His eyes gleamed and his lips lingered on her lips. She knew he was recalling her kiss this morning. And just a look at her lips sent her thoughts scattering. What were they talking about? Oh, yeah.

"What? That I wind up in trouble?" Quite suddenly his opinion mattered…a good deal. She was impulsive sometimes and she liked to consider herself a free spirit, however, she wasn't a loose cannon by any means. "Less than you might think."

The light changed and they were on their way again. "So why would I think you get into trouble a lot? Wait." His tone was teasing but there was an underlying note of seriousness. "Maybe because you go around kissing men you don't know? Hmmm."

"It's not a habit," she said with a laugh.

His grin was slightly lopsided, which was rather endearing in a man so structured and organized. "Do you realize you now have G.I.'s lining up to knock you down so you'll kiss them?"

She shrugged. "Occasionally my mouth does get me into trouble."

"Just curious, Eden, but why'd you kiss me this morning?"

"I guess it does actually beg an explanation, but you may think it's kind of strange."

"Baby, it can't be any stranger than you laying one on me in battalion headquarters' hallway."

Baby. Some men used the term and it struck her as demeaning or overly familiar. She was sure Mitch Dugan didn't use the term often. And coming from him it was hot. During their entire conversation, there'd been an awareness, a tension stretching between them, wrapping around them. It jumped to the forefront now.

"Okay," she said. "Here goes. You reminded me of someone, really something—a statue in my garden. Hey, it's not every day that a woman literally runs into a Roman god lookalike."

"You kissed me today in the hallway because I look like a garden statue. I'm not sure whether that would make or ruin my reputation." He could say whatever he wanted to but he was flattered. "Which god?"

"Mercury, messenger of the gods."

"So I look like this statue?"

Three days and counting. If she was going to flirt, she was going to flirt boldly. Going for it, meant *really* going for it. Eden didn't believe in half measures. "I can only vouch for the face because he's naked and you aren't. At least not yet."

"Baby," he said as he pulled into the restaurant parking lot. "I can see where your mouth could get you in all kinds of trouble."

6

MITCH LOOKED AT THE WOMAN sitting across from him sipping a sweet tea and looking around the restaurant in obvious appreciation.

She had him tied up in knots like he'd never been tied up before. And the hell of it was, he kind of liked it. Mitch knew for certain he felt more energized and alive than he'd ever felt before, and he'd been in some combat situations where his adrenaline had definitely been flowing. Maybe her particular brand of crazy was catching.

She turned her midnight-blue eyes on him. "I like this place," she said.

"I had a feeling this was what you had in mind." Funny how he felt tapped into her. Even though they were obviously vastly different in some respects, he felt an indescribable connection to her. It was as if one kiss this morning had plugged him into her. But that kind of logic was no logic at all. "Raeleen's is an institution with the locals."

Raeleen's Rib Shack served the best damn fall-off-the-bone smoked ribs smothered in a peppery sauce that begged to be washed down with an ice cold sweet tea. Sides of coleslaw, Brunswick stew, French fried sweet potatoes and banana pudding rounded things out. Eden struck him as a woman who indulged in *whatever* she had an appetite for. "Every bite's homemade by Raeleen and her daughters Shirleen and Jolene." She leaned forward, listening intently to what he was saying. He knew these were the kind of details that would fascinate her…and it was heady stuff, being the object of her fascination. Damn. He needed help. "Every once in a while Raeleen's husband, Paul, will call out for Lena, just to mix things up." Eden laughed and everything inside him tightened. "They all answer to the nickname."

"That's exactly the kind of stuff I like to know." Bingo. Was he seducing her or was she seducing him? And did it really matter? "Do you come here often?"

"Maybe once a month, sometimes more." But he always came alone or with Murdoch and Tara. He'd never brought a date here. "So, you never said how you wound up working on the calendar project when you didn't want to."

"I left the decision to be decided by my friend Patti, a bottle of limocello and a deck of Tarot cards."

Okay. This wasn't exactly the way he ran his life, but he found himself more fascinated than anything. "Do you ever make normal, rational decisions?"

She narrowed her eyes at him across the red-and-white checked plastic table cloth. Her entire demeanor screamed, *don't screw with me*. Whatever and whoever she was, she had backbone in spades. "Just because my decision-making process is different than yours, it doesn't make me irrational."

"But you're telling me you took this project because you'd been drinking and playing around with Tarot cards. And you kissed a total stranger because he reminded you of a garden statue."

"What? Would you rather hear that I found you utterly irresistible?"

"That wouldn't make any more logical sense than the fact that I reminded you of a statue. How could you, in less than a minute, find me so irresistible?" And what the hell was he doing having this crazy conversation with her. Eden Walters Disease. He'd caught it apparently.

"Now that's disappointing."

She could turn him on more with just a look than any other woman could with full-body contact. "What?"

"Here I thought you were the perfect man. But you can't be if you don't believe in instant irresistibility."

Yet once again, Mitch found himself laughing. She was so talking trash. There was nothing perfect about him, but it was fun to hear her say it. She brought out a playfulness in him he'd never known he possessed. Hell, she even inspired him to flirt, something he'd never been good at. Tough, commanding, take-charge. These were all adjectives he'd heard used to describe him. But flirtatious and playful? Who knew, maybe he wasn't good at it now but this soldier was going to give it a try. "How often do you find men instantly irresistible?"

"Until today? Never." She leaned across the table and whispered, "Now's a good time to tell me you find me irresistible, too."

"That could be dangerous, couldn't it, Eden? If we found one another irresistible?"

Raeleen herself delivered a platter of ribs, with Jolene—Shirleen had a mole on her neck—following with the stew, sweet potatoes and coleslaw. "Y'all need anything else?"

"We're good," Mitch said. "Thanks."

Eden snagged a couple of ribs and one of the fried sweet potato wedges. "I thought Special Forces specialized in dangerous missions, Lieutenant Colonel." She licked her fingertip, sampling the rib sauce. "Yum. Spicy but not too hot."

Wham! Sensation slammed him and shot straight to his crotch. And he suddenly knew he'd never been in more dangerous territory.

He took a long swallow of iced tea to cool down. "There are some things you're just not trained to handle."

"Maybe. But I get the feeling you're equipped to take on just about anything." She nibbled at the end of a meaty sauce-coated rib and his body responded with a strictly male, physical response. Watching her eat ribs might very well kill him tonight. But it would be a helluva way to go.

Somewhere in the dim recesses of the part of his brain that still held on to a shred of sanity, he remembered that she wasn't just any woman. She was the daughter of a very powerful man. One who could impact Mitch's career and not necessarily in a good way.

"Just about anything…except for pissed off brigadier generals."

"I'm a big girl, Mitch."

Damn it! That rib was far too phallic. He didn't need any reminders she was all grown up. That was obvious. A bead of sweat broke out on his neck.

"How would your father feel about you consorting with a soldier?"

"I have no idea. I've never consorted before…with a soldier, that is. Of course, I've consorted."

So, he was equally uncharted territory for her? "Not even a date?"

"Nope. I've always steered clear. It seemed like a good policy."

"But now…"

"Some rules are meant to broken. At least, on a temporary basis."

He'd be lying if he said that didn't notch the whole thing up a level for him. She was potent enough on her own, but to know he was the one who inspired her to break her own rule jacked him up even further. "Why does that not surprise me about you?"

"Let me guess. You're a rules-all-the-way kind of guy."

"You say that as if it's a bad thing." He was getting better at this flirting stuff—and his jeans were getting tighter and tighter.

"I suppose it's all a moot point if you don't find me irresistible, now, isn't it?" She put the cleaned bone on her plate.

"Did I say that?"

"You don't have to. We're still sitting here, aren't we?"

"You're not subtle, are you?"

"Almost never."

It didn't matter who her father was. It didn't matter that she'd be leaving in three days. It didn't matter that she was the last woman he should fall into bed with. He accepted what a part of him had known since that slow slide up his body this morning and that knock-him-for-a-loop kiss. He couldn't ignore—or resist—this thing between him and Eden Walters.

"Jolene, I'll take the check now."

SHE SHOULD BE NERVOUS. She should be mortified that she was about to hop into bed with a man she'd just met this morning. Instead, she was simply ready.

As if to confirm the rightness of what they were about to do, he reached down and grasped her hand in his. There was something infinitely touching in the simplicity of that gesture, in the respect he offered simply by holding her hand.

The streetlights glowed in the parking lot and he steered her around a pothole as he escorted her to her side of the Bronco. She was independent and she certainly managed to look out for herself, but she liked his gallantry, his attentiveness.

"Your place or mine?" he asked.

Gallant, yes. Suave, no. She laughed.

"I guess that did sound like a cliché."

"Just a little. Mine." There was something about the impartiality of a hotel room that was less intimidating than the intimacy of a house. His home. The truth of the matter was, contrarily she didn't want to fill in too many blanks about him. *Because you could get wrapped up in him way too fast and where would that leave you,* a reckoning voice whispered in her ear. Yep, quick in and out.

Silence settled between them and butterflies took off in her stomach. "Would you let me photograph you?" she said.

He cut her a quick glance. There was a lot less traffic heading back toward the hotel than there had been traveling out to Raeleen's.

"I thought you didn't want to photograph me for the calendar?"

"I don't. You aren't calendar material. This would be private. Just for me. You don't have to let me know now. Just think about it."

"Are you always so shy and retiring?"

Hmm. Eden got the impression that her arrogant, in-command paratrooper was slightly nervous and filling the silence with small talk.

"Believe it or not, I was as a kid. But when you move as often as we did, you either drown in shyness or you learn to swim. I'm a swimmer."

"I'd say captain of the swim team," he said.

Ah, there was his arrogant smile coming through. She found the different facets of Mitch Dugan fascinating. For a man who lived his life in black and white, he was a riveting mix of shades of gray.

"Was that a joke?"

"I have the occasional lapse."

They turned into the hotel entrance and Mitch parked in a remote corner of the parking lot.

"Take off your seat belt and slide this way a little bit."

"Don't you want to go inside?"

"Not yet." He shifted to face her in his seat. It was dark and intimate in the front of his truck and she felt the same surge of nervous anticipation she'd felt as a teenager when she went parking with her boyfriend her senior year. Only this was much, much better because both of them had some experience under their belts. He leaned in and his breath was warm against her skin. "Any good soldier knows you need to check out the lay of the land before you move in. The more you know, the better the outcome." He intertwined the fingers of his left hand with her right and her pulse kicked into hyper speed. "And I always aim for optimal outcome."

She returned his banter, her fingers curling against his warm hand. "Do you always approach sex like a military operation?"

"You have to go with what you know." He nuzzled the line of her jaw, his whiskers a faint scrape against her sensitive skin. "If you change your mind, all you have to do is say so. No explanation required. I'll drive you to the front entrance, drop you off and we can forget this ever happened."

"That's generous."

"No. Your offer is generous. I'm just trying to be fair."

He feathered his fingers along the line of her jaw and her breath caught in her throat. He smoothed a finger over the fullness of her bottom lip. "I've thought about your mouth all day long."

Sweet mercy. One light touch and that dulcet low murmur and her panties were soaked.

"Me, too. I mean thought about your mouth, not mine."

"I wanted to do this…" His touch was gossamer light as he skimmed his palm down the length of her neck to the hollow that led to her collarbone.

Oh. My. God. She hadn't expected just a simple touch to quiver through her.

He cupped her jaw in his hand, sliding his fingers past the sensitive spot just below her ear. "Your skin is just as soft as it looks."

She had never wanted anything as badly as she wanted his mouth on hers. His moss-green eyes were intense in the shadowed cab. She slid her arm over his shoulder and wrapped her fingers around the back of his neck.

"Ki—"

He interrupted what was going to be a *Kiss me* directive. "No. I'm in charge of this mission."

What could have come across as peremptory just sounded hot. *Really* hot. He was a man used to being in charge. If he wanted to take the lead now, she was good with that.

His breath fanned against her cheek, her mouth and then finally his lips found hers. He tasted like a combination of sweet and spicy, sweet tea and peppery barbeque sauce. It was a sampling kiss, followed by another, then another. She sighed into him. This was even better than this morning.

He kissed her harder and she kissed him back with equal intensity. She lost track of everything except the mingling of his breath with hers, the sweep of his tongue caressing hers, the rasp of his calloused fingers against her skin.

An ache, hot and sweet and wet, blossomed inside her. His groan echoed into her mouth and she sent it back to him.

His breath was gratifyingly uneven when he pulled away. In a surprisingly tender gesture, he rested his forehead against hers.

"So, do I stay or go?"

"You're not much of a reconnaissance man, soldier, if you have to ask."

NEITHER ONE OF THEM SPOKE as they crossed the lobby to the elevators. When the doors closed behind them, enclosing them in the elevator's confines, the sexual tension in the air was almost tangible.

"What floor?"

"Five."

Mitch pushed the button and stood at parade rest. He didn't dare touch her again until they were in her room. Just kissing her, the press of her hand against his neck, the softness of her skin beneath his fingertips had him trembling.

That had never happened before—the feeling that he was teetering on the brink of moving beyond himself, not quite in control. And the smart thing to do would've been to drop her at the front door and get the hell home. But he simply couldn't walk away from her, which was all the more reason to. But he couldn't.

He wanted to know what it felt like to be sheathed inside her, to be buried in her warmth and exuberance. And it wasn't just about getting laid—that could happen on any given night at pretty much any bar in town. He was a decent-looking guy and the ladies seemed to like him. No. This was about her. And him. About the fact that he'd wanted to be inside her since she'd journeyed up his body in that sensuous slide this morning. And that the thought of McElhaney touching her left him wanting to break something—preferably McElhaney's face.

Eden fished her key card out of her purse.

The elevator dinged open. "It's this way," she said,

turning left down the hallway, leading the way. The crazy thought flitted through his head that right now, he'd follow her to Hell and back. She was a frantic need inside him. All the more reason to retreat...all the more reason he couldn't.

"Seems nice enough," Mitch said, glancing around the hallway, noting the layout and the exit.

"It is. I stay in a lot of hotels and this is one of the nicer ones I've seen. It doesn't have that funky smell some of them do."

"You travel a lot?"

"Enough that I'm always glad to get back home." She slid the card into the door and the green light lit up. Pushing open the door, she quipped, "Here it is. Home sweet home, at least for the next few days."

He automatically scanned the room.

To the right, the suite offered a full-size refrigerator, microwave, dishwasher and as much counter space as someone with limited culinary capabilities might require. To the left sat a dining table with two chairs. The rest of the room offered a desk, a sleeper sofa, a television and a fireplace angled into one wall. The bedroom lay through a doorway to the right of the fireplace.

Mitch hung the Do Not Disturb sign on the outside, closed the door, clicked the dead bolt into place and turned to face Eden. "We'll take this as slow...or as fast...as you want to take it."

"We might want to slow it down a bit." For all that she'd been forward and bold, she looked a little unsure of herself. Obviously, she didn't do this type of thing often, if ever. He might not be good at flirting but he knew all about being a leader. So he took charge.

He crossed the room, turned a corner lamp on low, walked back over and killed the overhead.

He held out his hand. "Come here."

She put her hand in his and he led her to the sofa in the main room. He sat down, pulling her down beside him. "Where were we?"

Her smile rocked his world as she leaned into him. "Something must've distracted you, Lieutenant Colonel." She trailed kisses up the side of his neck, nipping at the tip of his ear. "You were conducting a re-connaissance mission."

"Then let me get back on task."

7

EDEN DIDN'T EVEN TRY TO STIFLE her moan as she tugged his shirt free of the waist of his jeans. *Finally.*

She kneaded the muscles rippling along his back. His skin was warm and supple until she encountered a ridge of scar tissue. A warrior's mark. Later. She'd ask later where he earned that.

He nibbled his way along the ridge of her collarbone and up the sensitive line of her neck. Oh. My. God.

"That feels…so…good."

He laughed softly, his breath warm against her highly-charged skin. "Does it? Does it feel as good as this?"

Like a magician casting a spell over her, he trailed a matching set of kisses up the other side of her neck. Yes…

"Hmm. That might even feel better."

"Really? Then what about this?" He scraped his teeth over the back of her neck and sensation shot straight to her core followed by a rush of wetness.

She gasped. "Oh…yes…."

"Put your arms around my neck," he said.

She did. Though blindly following orders went against everything she believed in, she had a feeling this would be to her benefit.

In one smooth motion he stood, scooping her up in his arms. "Do you mind if we move to the bed? There's a whole lot more room there."

"Be my guest."

She felt his belly muscles clench against her hip. She'd thought she couldn't be any more turned on. But when he took her in his arms, she realized she could. She was.

He crossed the room, carrying her as if she weighed no more than a sack of groceries—which God and her bathroom scales knew she did. He deposited her on the bed, kneeling.

"Take off your shirt," she said. He wasn't the only one who could issue orders.

He complied in short order, pulling his shirt up, over and off his torso. There was certainly no doubt he was Special Forces, not that there ever had been.

"Oh…"

He was…in short order…ripped. Shoulders, arms, chest, belly—all muscle and taut dark skin with hair scattered over his chest and down the ridged plane of his belly. A man in prime condition. Her Mercury.

An arrogant smile curved his mouth. He had every right to be arrogant. He obviously worked damn hard to be in that shape. Any man who passed the rigorous training he had, and maintained that training on a regular basis should be proud of what he had. Which was why he could pick her up and carry her across the room as if her 150 pounds was of no consequence.

"And I thought you were beautiful before…" she said.

He shook his head, as if she constantly confounded him. "Men aren't beautiful."

Eden hooked her finger in the edge of his jeans and tugged him toward her. "Honey, that is all a matter of perspective."

He lowered himself to lie beside her and brushed his hand over her forehead, along the curve and hollow of her cheekbone. His touch, sensuous, reverent had her shivering inside. "*You* are beautiful. I wasn't quite sure what hit me this morning and then I looked down and…" He outlined her lips with this finger. "I'm supposed to be prepared for anything. I wasn't, however, prepared for a woman with midnight-blue eyes, an irresistible mouth, gorgeous legs and sexy red heels."

"Soldier, you know exactly what to say," she said, exploring the texture of his skin with her hand, testing the springiness of his chest hair with her fingers.

"I've wanted to do this all day." He pushed her back against the mattress and licked her bottom lip. It was quite possibly one of the most erotic things she'd ever had done to her. "And this…" He brushed his mouth over hers in a butterfly kiss, stealing her breath. All thought vanished. Only the sensation of his lips, his breath, his scent, his body heat remained. Then he caught her lower lip in between his teeth and nipped at it. A gentle, insistent tugging. Her nipples hardened even further against her bra as if each nibble, each caress was wired through to the very core of her.

"If—" he took another lick along her lip "I do anything—" he scraped his teeth against the sensitive flesh he'd just licked "—you don't like, tell me."

"So far, you've got a one-hundred percent approval rating."

And she figured if he liked doing that to her, chances were he'd like it done to him. She pushed him to his back—which he allowed because she obviously couldn't push him anywhere he didn't want to go. Good thing they both wanted to go to the same place.

"Baby…"

"Hmm?" she murmured, plying her tongue along his gorgeously chiseled lip. And then she couldn't resist. She teased the tip of her tongue along the faint cleft in his chin. She wasn't quite sure why that was so sexy, but it was. The faint scrape of whiskers, the slight taste of salt against the tip of her tongue.

"Take your shirt off," he said, in a husky tone. "Please," he tacked on.

And there was something very arousing about that *please*. She was certain Lieutenant Colonel Mitch Dugan didn't ask for things. He ordered and expected his directive to be carried out. But she knew with a certainty that he didn't *ask*. If she hadn't been thoroughly enchanted with him already, his *please* would have sealed the deal. He could get pretty much anything out of her with that entreaty. Well, he could pretty much get anything out of her anyway, but...

"Since you said please," she said with a teasing smile.

"Is that all it takes?" He raised his arms, pillowing his head on his hands.

Eden swallowed hard. Trip another trigger for her. That thatch of dark hair in his armpits, the swell and bulge of bicep and tricep... Dear God, she was in imminent danger of just melting into a puddle of desire right beside him. Discovering his dry sense of humor had been a nice surprise today. It was an even nicer surprise to have it turn up in the bedroom. *Is that all it takes?*

"There's only one way to find out, isn't there?" She edged her shirt up her waist, then suffered an attack of cold feet. He was rock-solid and ripped. He was sculpted and perfect. She wasn't. She was rounded and the ugly truth was she looked a whole lot better with her clothes on than without, considering that she had a midriff roll going and her thighs could be a whole lot tighter.

His hiss of indrawn breath broke the room's silence. It wasn't a horrified gasp. It was the sound of a man who liked what he saw. Obviously he appreciated curves and softness. All her insecurities vanished beneath the appreciation glittering in his green eyes.

So she continued—slowly, deliberately edging her shirt up, her skin sensitized to the slide of material over her, past her shoulders and over her head. Cool air settled on her skin, making her even more aroused, if that was possible.

"Red—" his voice rasped and it had the same effect on her as his calloused fingers against her skin "—is a good color on you. I should've known this morning when I saw those shoes. Are your panties red, too?"

From the bulge in the front of his jeans, he liked the color. A lot.

She edged off of the bed and slipped off the flats she'd worn earlier, then slowly slid the zipper of her jeans down.

She worked the jeans over her hips with a little more wiggle than was necessary but he seemed to enjoy the show. Then she stepped out of her pants and into the red heels she'd tossed over by the dresser earlier.

Eden strolled over to the side of the bed. "A matching set."

He unfolded his hands from beneath his head and reached for her. "Come here. Please."

HE COULDN'T THINK. HE COULD barely breathe. It was as if everything in him, about him, was focused on her. It had been this way all day long, from the very moment she'd bounced off of him and onto her lovely ass in that hallway. How he could want her, feel this way about a woman he'd just met less than eighteen hours earlier was…confounding. But then again, everything about her was confounding.

"You wanted me here. I'm here."

He wrapped his hands around her hips and lifted her onto the bed next to him. "No. I wanted you here." Her skin was warm, soft silk beneath his hands. "And if—no, when—everything else comes off, please keep the red heels on."

"Is that an order?"

"It's whatever you want it to be—an order, a request, a desperate man's plea."

"You don't look desperate to me. Take off your pants, Lieutenant Colonel."

"That sounded suspiciously like a direct order."

"It's whatever you want it to be."

He stood and unbuttoned his jeans. "It doesn't really matter, does it?"

"Not really." She settled back on her elbows, half sitting, half reclining, her eyelids lowering to a sexy half-mast, watching him. Waiting. "Take your time."

He slowly slid his zipper down. She'd given him a show, so he'd return the favor. He knew, without being arrogant, that he was in good shape. And he knew from the look in her eyes that she appreciated what good shape he was in. He couldn't quite manage the hip wiggle she did, and he had to admit he felt moderately ridiculous even thinking about giving it a try. "I'm a soldier, not a stripper."

From her vantage point on the bed, Eden grinned. "I think you might have a second career in your future."

"I think not." Nevertheless he turned his back to her and gave it a shot. He imagined being inside her and instead of an in-out thrust, he'd grind against her.

Behind him, the sharp hiss of her indrawn breath filled the room's silence. "Oh, my," she said.

He pivoted on one foot, turning to face her in his briefs. Her eyes skimmed over his chest, down his belly, to his erection. Her eyes widened. "Oh. My."

He hooked his thumbs in the elastic waistband and paused, giving her the opportunity to tell him to slow down. Instead a smile that could only be considered an invitation to keep going blossomed over her face and lit her eyes.

He slid his underwear down, stepped out of them, and straightened. "Don't move," she ordered, a rich, husky note in her voice. "I'm taking a mental picture of you." Her gaze slid over him as if she was studying his contours and planes. It was the next best thing to feeling her fingers against his skin. His penis lengthened, hardened even more at the heat in her eyes.

"Are you through looking?"

"No. But I'm a multitasker. I'd like to taste and touch at the same time."

He braced one knee on the bed and paused before joining her on the mattress. He traced his index finger along the delicate blue vein running along the top of her foot, past the indention of her ankle to the curve of her calf. Beneath his fingertip, she shivered and his entire body tightened in response.

She reached for him at the same time he lowered himself beside her, flesh against flesh except for the scraps of her panties and bra. As much as he wanted her, he wanted all of her. It wouldn't be enough to thrust between her thighs and be done. He wanted to know the soft skin behind her knees, the taste of the indent of her back. He wanted to explore and capture and know her sparkle, her joy.

So he set about doing just that.

EVERYTHING CAME DOWN TO HER, to him. Eden gave herself over to the feel of his hands on her shoulders, her belly, her thighs. The texture of his skin against hers. The hair of his chest, the heaviness of his erection against her hip, his mouth teasing, taunting, nuzzling, nibbling down her neck, her chest. She sucked in a heated breath when he slid her bra straps over and down her shoulders.

She arched her back, offering herself to him. His breath was warm against the tops of her breasts. The ache inside her intensified to a steady thrum. She wanted his hands and beautiful mouth on her. She wanted this man so like the god in her garden to feast on her, to make her a part of him.

Mitch lowered his head until his mouth hovered just above her nipple and she ached for the feel of him against her flesh. He teased his tongue against her tip and sure, swift heat coursed from her breast to her core, intensifying the moisture gathered between her thighs.

He laved, nipped and suckled one breast and then the other. Eden wrapped her leg around his bare hip and buttocks, pulling him closer until his penis nudged against her wet satin panties. Her hips lifted, bringing her mound into exquisite contact with his erection.

Skin on skin, the ripple of muscles beneath her hands mesmerized her as she stroked and kneaded his back. And then, suddenly, her bra was gone and he was tearing open and donning a condom. Her heart pounded and her breath came in sharp, quick gasps. She reached up and pulled his mouth back down to hers, bring his hard hair-roughened chest into contact with her breasts.

He raised his head and broke their kiss long enough to ask, "Panties on and pushed aside or off?"

"On and pushed aside."

She gasped into his mouth as he slowly nudged into her, filling her with male heat, stretching her. He set up a slow, steady rhythm and with each thrust she climbed a little further, until she felt herself beginning to shatter inside. Amazingly, he pushed her to climb a little higher, to hold on a little tighter. And when she finally came, it was the most incredible sexual experience she'd ever had.

8

MITCH MENTALLY STEADIED himself as he excused himself to the bathroom to clean up. Once that was out of the way, he splashed bracing cold water onto his face. He considered himself a thoughtful lover. He never jumped right in unless that's what the woman of the hour wanted. He didn't finish first. He was a man who knew supreme self-control and discipline. All his training had invariably touched every aspect of his life, including his sex life. With Eden Walters, however, his discipline and self-control had gone AWOL. They'd had a rhythm together, as if the two of them were in some kind of silent, weird sync. And it was a damn good thing. Mitch wasn't altogether sure that he could have waited had her orgasm not been on pace with his own. And that had never, ever happened before.

He should walk back out there, thank her, pull on his clothes and head on home. He'd come. She'd come. All was well on the let's-hook-up front. That's what he should do. But it sure as hell wasn't what he wanted to do. And it wasn't what he was *going* to do.

Because, damn it all to hell and back, he'd just had

her…and he wanted her again. It was like going on a recon mission and gathering good intel, but knowing if you went back in, there was still a lot left to discover. And since he'd never been one to bullshit himself, he wanted to prove that he could have sex with her and still keep control. So, she'd screwed with his self-discipline once. It wouldn't happen again. He needed to know it couldn't happen again. And he'd prove it, although the thought occurred to him that he might screw himself to do just that. At least it'd be a hell of a way to go.

He opened the bathroom door and flipped the light switch off. Eden had turned on one of the bedside lamps and stood in front of the window wearing those red heels and a short cream-colored robe knotted at her waist. The faint red of her panties showed through the robe's light color. She looked over her shoulder, an almost-shy smile on her face as if she were suffering from a case of the awkward morning-afters. Just when he thought he had her figured out, she surprised him.

Instinctively, automatically he returned her smile, crossing the room to stand behind her. He lightly bracketed her shoulders in his hands and God help him, a shiver ran through him at the hint of heat and sweet supple skin beneath the silky fabric. "Hey."

Damn. That was it? That was all he could come up with? Yep. Because her body heat seemed to shimmer all around him, drawing him like a light in a dark tunnel. And her scent that now carried his scent, as well…. Yep, *hey* was all he could come up with. Control, Dugan, control.

"Hey, yourself."

Did she want him to go? Stay? He couldn't read her. He rubbed slow circles against her shoulders with his palms. "What are you looking at?"

She leaned back into him. Signal received. He could stay. "Fayetteville. Do you like it here?"

He encircled her waist with his arms, pulling her into closer contact, her satin-covered curves fitting against him just right. He bent his head, her hair teasing against his face, and nuzzled her neck, inhaling her scent, hungry for another taste of her. "I like it here, and here, and here."

An unsteady note colored her low, husky laugh. "That wasn't what I meant." She raised one arm and brushed her fingers over his head, curling them around his neck. "But I think I prefer your conversational thread."

He used his teeth to tug her robe off her shoulder, exposing the top half of her breast. "How do you like it here?" he asked, nibbling his way over her skin.

She pressed her ass more firmly against his crotch, a small gasp hissing from between her lips. "I like it."

He parted her robe slightly and slid his hands over the smooth soft skin of her belly while he continued to make love to her shoulder with his mouth. Damn but she felt good against him, beneath his hands. He lightly skimmed the line of her panties, tracing the outline of the scrap of red satin and lace, then moved past to grasp her thighs in his hands. He squeezed, careful not to be too hard. She moaned and wiggled against him. Continuing to squeeze her thighs, he pulled them slightly as if to open her up. Her breath came in short pants. Then he ran his thumb along the damp crotch of her panties and she jerked against him. She definitely liked that and he was all about pleasing her, all about driving her over the edge. As long as he stayed in control this time.

Neither one of them said a word. This was all about body language. He moved his thumb against her again and her soft moan told him all he needed to know. He slid his finger beneath the edge of her panties. He rimmed her, carefully avoiding her clit and her slick wet opening. Teasing her, toying with her. Dammit she felt good. And his fully erect dick was now happily nestled against her robe between the cheeks of her ass. She rocked, as if torn between wanting his dick or his fingers. He teased his fingertip through the soft curls between her thighs, touching her, but not where she wanted. She arched against him, like a heat-seeking missile tracking its target. He deftly avoided giving her what she wanted. Not yet. Only this was turning into an equally sweet torture for him, as well.

He slid his left hand up and cupped her breast, toying with her erect nipple, notching both of them higher and higher. Finally, he skated his other finger along her slick wet folds until he found her swollen nubbin. He eased a finger into her, his thumb teasing against her clit and she mewled in the back of her throat, a wanton sound that sent him skating dangerously close to his own edge.

"Mitch." It was more a gasp than an actual enunciation of his name. She grasped his wrist and pulled his finger out of her. She turned to face him, her nipples hard. She drew his hand to her mouth and licked his finger that had been inside her and then took it in her mouth and sucked on it.

He felt as if he'd just had a grenade go off beside him. With a sweet smile she turned, her hand still on his wrist, taking him with her. Two steps and she was at the armchair next to the window. Moments later, her panties fell to the floor. Another second passed and she was on the chair, her back to him, her legs on the arms, showing him the gate to Paradise. She leaned forward, resting her arms on the chair back and looked over her shoulder.

"I think we're both ready to complete this mission, Lieutenant Colonel."

THE FOLLOWING MORNING, Eden was ready and waiting in the hotel lobby at precisely 6:00 a.m. Mitch had gone home around four to shower and change. He was swinging by to pick her up and drive her into the base. They'd get there just as the first round of early morning physical training ended. She hoped to finish up her candidate list and start preliminary shooting that afternoon, which should work out well from a lighting standpoint. She'd like to fire off several shots at the ropes section of the obstacle course....

"Ready?"

Eden jumped. She'd been so lost in mentally planning her day, she hadn't seen him enter the lobby. But he was certainly here now. Every inch of her was aware of all six plus feet of him. Too bad every inch of her had to be content with merely looking. While the nights might be their own, during the days, they both had to do their jobs and maintain some measure of circumspection. No looks, no touches, no nothing.

"Ready."

He held the door for her and she preceded him out into the chilly October predawn. With two sure strides he beat her to the truck door and opened it for her. "Thanks," she murmured.

Before she had her seat belt clicked into place, he was in the driver's seat and they were on their way. "So, we need to discuss the game plan for the day," he said, now all business.

They hadn't talked about it last night, or rather early this morning before he left, but she'd known they'd have to play by the rules of the military once again. Still, she was taken slightly aback. "Sure," she said, as abrupt as him.

"Eden." He stared straight ahead at the road. "It's better this way. It's going to be damn hard to go through the day not touching you." He laughed and it wasn't as if he was amused. "It took every ounce of discipline I had not to haul you upstairs and back to bed just now, saying to hell with whether or not we're on time. And if we start talking about last night or this morning when I was leaving—" that had been incredible, as well. "—or thinking about tonight—" he scrubbed a hand over his close-cropped hair "—then I have no idea how I'm going to get through the day. It's already going to be hard enough. So I can't think about it. At least, I'm going to do my damnedest not to think about it. Therein lies madness."

He was right. She'd known it but it was all the better for hearing him say it. "You're right. I thought about dragging you upstairs, as well."

"Stop right there. Under no circumstances should you tell me what you planned to do when we got there." Although there was dry amusement in his voice, there was also no mistaking the strain.

She found it gratifying to know the well-disciplined Lieutenant Colonel Mitch Dugan found it as difficult to keep his hands off of her as she found it to keep her hands off of him.

Six hours later, she was dying a slow death of wanting for Mitch even as she wrapped up her final candidate choice. "Thanks. I think you'll be great. We'll pull you in tomorrow morning," she told the young man with mocha skin, liquid dark eyes and a physique that would leave the women buying the calendar checking his month over and over again. At least that's what her trained eye told her. Personally, she couldn't work up a good womanly appreciation. Her appreciation was firmly tied up elsewhere.

She'd spent the morning culling and verifying her final candidates. Eden had never, ever had a difficult time focusing on work. Behind the camera was where she loved to be, where she lost herself and found herself at the same time. But not today. She'd been totally out of sync with her work and totally tuned into Mitch Dugan. Dammit to hell, if the man shifted weight from one foot to the other, she knew it. What the heck was wrong with her? Sure, he'd been good in bed—well, that was something of a gross understatement—but so had other guys. She hadn't been totally wrapped up in them the way she found herself wrapped up in Mitch.

This had been the longest day of her life, and it was only half over. She wanted her work to be done. She wanted to drive off base and leave all the protocol and rules and regulations behind and go back to her hotel and leave no inch of his body unexplored.

"Do you want to grab some quick lunch?" Mitch asked when they got back to his Bronco.

"Just something fast. I'd like to get as much done today as possible. The weather's good, the lighting is perfect. I'd like to get as much shooting done as possible. You've got our first wave scheduled?"

"They should be at the obstacle course at 1300 hours."

Mitch's efficiency hadn't surprised her. But his willingness to take on what his assistant usually handled without any indication that such menial tasks were beneath him had impressed her. He was arrogant and self-assured but, unlike so many men she'd met, especially at his level of rank, he didn't seem to have an inflated sense of self.

"Thanks for all of your help. I know this wasn't your assignment of choice but you've seen to it that things go smoothly."

He smiled and there was a glimmer of what had passed between them last night in his eyes. "The smoother the day goes, the sooner we finish."

"Do you have plans this evening?"

"I've got a mission."

"Another recon?"

"There is that. The better the intel, the more thoroughly you can do the job in the end."

"Are you always so thorough?"

"If you're going to do a job, you might as well do it right."

"You get full marks, Lieutenant Colonel for doing *everything* right."

A brief flash of a grin that was a heart-stopping mix of self-assured commander and boyishness lit his face. "Just wait."

A shot of adrenaline coursed through her. "Is that a warning?"

"No, ma'am. Consider it a promise."

9

"WHERE DO YOU LIVE?" EDEN asked from the passenger seat as they were leaving the base. "An apartment? Condo?"

"I bought a house last year. It's a good investment and I like being in my own space at the end of the day." What was it about her that she was so damn easy to be with in one respect but so damn hard to be with in another. Because his normal routine was totally shot to hell when he was around her. The smart thing to do would be not to be around her at the end of the day but once again, smart didn't seem to be an option for him. Damn it all, he couldn't stay away from her. He'd never met a woman like her. He reassured himself that this fascination would end soon enough. She'd go her way, he'd go his and they'd have some damn hot memories. He'd never met a woman who affected him the way she did and he was equally sure he'd never meet another. Eden Walters was a once-in-a-lifetime experience— one that would be out of his life in a couple of days. That made her safe—even if she was Brigadier General

Max Walters's daughter. Hell, she was no more eager to reveal their relationship to her parents than he was.

She looked at him in surprise. "You just don't strike me as the suburban type."

Mitch grinned. It was a nice change to be the one surprising her. "I happen to like yard work. I can mow with the best of them."

She laughed. He liked to hear her laugh. And it was better still when he was the one who caused it. "Now, that I'd like to see. Mercury behind a lawn mower."

Mitch rolled his eyes at the whole Mercury thing, but he had to admit, it was pretty flattering stuff to have a woman—correction, *this* woman—compare him to a Roman god.

"Well, I'm not going to break out the mower but we could swing by my house later. That is, if you want to." Where the hell had that come from? It wasn't because he *wanted* her to see his house.

"I'm a woman and I'm eternally curious. Of course, I want to."

That was yet another thing he liked about her. He dealt with layers all day. Although things seemed straightforward in the military there were always strategies and some measure of subterfuge involved. As far as he could tell, that wasn't the case with this woman. If she thought it, she said it. If she wanted it, she asked. No games. No pretense. Hell, he almost worried about how vulnerable that left her. Didn't she know how dangerous it was to leave herself so open? She brought out protective instincts he didn't even know he possessed. He wanted to caution her, but he was pretty sure it would fall on deaf ears. Besides, it was such a refreshing change to the world he lived in that it would be a shame to mess with it. What she needed was a buffer. Someone to have her back when that openness left her vulnerable. But it damn sure wasn't him. Nope. She needed someone, but not him.

"I will get a tour, right?" she said.

He shrugged. "It's nothing fancy, but sure. And don't even ask me to bring out the mower."

"Believe it or not, soldier, there are other things I'd rather you bring out…"

Whoosh! In two seconds the banked, smoldering fire that had been between them roared to full-burn status. "Are you propositioning me, Ms. Walters?"

"Damn straight I am, Lieutenant Colonel."

"I like the way you think."

"But you haven't even heard my proposal. How do you know whether you want to accept?"

Oh, he was reading her. When she wasn't working, the woman had a playful streak a mile wide. He'd been surprised at the discipline and focus she brought to her job. Actually, the focus hadn't been that much of a surprise because the woman knew exactly what she wanted in the bedroom, too. Her mixture of playfulness and intensity had made for some incredible, mind-blowing sex.

"Then maybe you should outline your proposal."

This had been the longest day of his life, bar none. Being around her but not touching her, being on guard all day against a look or nuance that would give away the attraction churning inside him was killing him. As crazy as it seemed, today had been tougher and demanded more willpower than any day he'd spent in Special Forces training. How was that for a kick in the ass? Eden Walters demanded more endurance than the toughest program the U.S. Army offered.

And now they were almost at his house and that incredible willpower was no longer required. He was ready to play hard…with her. "Better yet, I think I need the details."

She reached across the seat and lightly placed her hand on his right thigh. Bingo. Instant rush of blood to his dick, a sudden surge of absolute need to have her touch him, to touch her, intimately.

"I think that's an excellent starting point," he said.

"But I haven't even said anything yet." She slid her hand higher.

"Body language, baby. I'm hearing you and I like what you're saying."

He could feel the heat of her laser gaze on his crotch. "I like what you're saying as well, Lieutenant Colonel." She stroked his inner thigh. "There are other tools I'm much more interested in seeing than your lawn mower." She used one finger to trace the ridge of his erection where it strained against his BDU's.

Even with his uniform and underwear between his penis and her forefinger, her touch rocked him.

Mitch wrapped his hands tighter around the steering wheel. "I think that can be arranged."

"I'm a team player so I'll be glad to help you take it out." She stroked him again. "What do you think so far?"

"A most excellent proposal. What comes next?"

What followed was a descriptive scenario where she told him exactly what she planned to do to him, all while her fingers continued to tease and taunt him into insanity.

He was damn near at his breaking point when he uttered a one-word command, "Enough." If she continued talking in that sultry voice, with her clever little hand stroking him to madness, he was going to come before he even got the truck pulled into the driveway.

She rested her fingers on his thigh, close but not touching him. It was a more diabolical torture than anything he'd learned in the military. She wiggled in the seat and he *knew* she was wet. *For him.* It was heady stuff, no pun intended.

"Enough?" Her fingers played against his thigh muscle. "Are you sure you don't need to hear more before you accept or decline?"

"Baby, if I *hear* any more, your proposal is going to be shot to hell before we even get started."

"Then I guess my lips are sealed…until we get to your house."

He couldn't get there fast enough.

"So, HOW MUCH TROUBLE WILL that get you into?" Eden asked, as the police car pulled out past them. She only felt marginally guilty. It really was kind of funny.

"I'll probably just get a talk about setting a good example. Speeding in a residential neighborhood isn't cool, but it's not a DUI or some of the other stuff that goes down."

"Hope that didn't ruin your—"

He cut her off. "Not by a long shot. I'm still up for your proposal."

She looked at his crotch. Yes, he was. Now that was impressive. After a speeding ticket and a hefty fine, his pump was still primed. She was definitely ready, but then that seemed to be her perpetual state around Mitch. He might look like her Mercury statue in lots of respects but Mitch was definitely superior to the Roman god in the packaging department.

He turned into a neighborhood and she marginally registered the neat lawns and tidy brick houses. Please let them get to his house soon. She was wound so tight she felt as if she might break through her own skin. Arousal was a tight fist clutching her. There was nothing tame or gentle about the way she wanted him. And it was only him she wanted. Not one of the hard bodies she'd photographed this afternoon, but this man with whom she'd felt a connection from the moment she'd seen him.

She slanted another hungry look at his crotch. While there was solid proof bulging at the front of his uniform that he needed her too, she also felt wave after wave of sexual tension radiating from him. She might be gone after tomorrow but for right now, Mitch Dugan wanted her. And by God, she planned to let him have her, six ways to Sunday.

He turned into a driveway and pulled into an open carport. Eden had her seat belt unlatched and her door open by the time he killed the engine. She stood beside him, not touching him while he unlocked the door. His body heat was like a magnet drawing her, his scent pulling her in, but she didn't dare get too close until they were safely on the other side of the door. She couldn't guarantee they wouldn't provide a shocking display for the neighborhood.

He had to try the key twice before he managed to turn the lock. Her Special Forces paratrooper wasn't quite as unflappable as he might appear. Then they were inside. The door had no sooner closed behind them than they were reaching for one another.

She linked her arms around his neck and stood on tiptoe to fit her crotch against the bulge in his. His mouth swooped onto hers and he caught her buttocks up in his broad hands, holding her more firmly still against his erection. She ground her hips against him and sucked his tongue into her mouth.

Slowly, deliberately she did to his tongue what she was about to do to his penis. He groaned into her mouth. She relinquished his tongue and pretended to pin him against the door as she nipped at the masculine column of his throat and reached between them to release his belt and unbutton his pants. She slipped her hand inside his open uniform to cup him through the thin cotton of his briefs. Her heart thumped against her ribs as she slid down his body, settling on her knees before him.

She leaned in and inhaled his unique scent. She carefully eased his briefs down over the length of his erection. God, he was beautiful. Springing long and sleek from a nest of dark brown hair, his penis curved slightly up. His sac hung heavy and full beneath.

She steadied herself with her hands on his hips and delicately traced the blue vein on the underside of his penis with the tip of her tongue. She felt him shudder beneath her hands and heard the hard rasp of his breathing before he uttered a rusty yes.

She caught the weight of his balls in her palm and held them as she rimmed his sleek, crowned head. She loved the scent of him, the taste of him, the feel of him.

Wrapping her other hand around his shaft she eased his length into her mouth, or as much as she could fit. She worked her tongue around and over him, enjoying knowing that she was pushing him to the brink.

He grew harder and his body increasingly tensed as she kissed and sucked and tongued him. "Stop," he said.

She looked up at him. Jaw clenched, green eyes glittering, he dragged her up his body. Before she could utter a word, he'd reversed positions and Eden was against the door. He reached into his pocket and pulled out a condom. While Mitch tore into the cellophane wrapper, she unzipped her pants and stepped out of them and her shoes. He rolled on the condom and she rolled off her panties. The air cool against the hot wet heat between her thighs made her shiver.

Still without a word passing between them, she wrapped her arms around his neck and one leg around his lean hips, opening herself to him.

He grasped the back of her thighs and lifted her up, then settled her just above his sheathed erection, teasing her, tempting her. Finally, inch by inch, he eased her down over his thick length until she swore she could feel him pressing past her womb to a secret place that had been waiting just for him. She gasped from the utter pleasure of having him stretch her, fill her. She lost herself in the sensations spinning through her.

"Yes. Yes. That's it…" He reached between them and found her clit with his thumb and there was no gradual build-up and release. Eden screamed as an orgasm like none she'd ever known before tore through her, the pleasure so intense it bordered on pain.

MITCH LAY IN HIS BED AND watched the moonlight filter over Eden's face and naked shoulder. After they'd christened the kitchen door, he'd shown her the house, thrown a couple of steaks on the grill, and they'd enjoyed dinner on his back deck. Ultimately, they'd wound up in his bed.

"What's on your agenda after you finish the calendar shoot? Do you have plans this weekend?"

"I'm just heading home after I do that family photo for Sergeant Sanchez. My schedule is open until next Wednesday when I'm flying to Denver for a week. Why? What did you have in mind?"

The idea had occurred to him earlier in the day when he was watching her work. "Do you think I could talk you into an assignment in between? Of course, I'd pay you your going rate."

She rolled onto her side. "Maybe. If you play your cards right, I might even give you a discount." She propped up on her elbow, the sheet dipping distractingly low on her left breast. "You've definitely got my interest."

He told her about his grandfather's birthday and the reunion with the remaining five members of their group. "I've got a feeling this could be the last time they all get together. Someone there will have a camera, but they won't capture it the way you would. It's about an hour and a half north of New Orleans. Could I talk you into taking photos of the old geezers?"

She was as quiet as he'd ever seen her. It was like watching the surface of a ripple-less pond. You knew the water was deep, but it was so still, you had no idea just how deep it was.

Her eyes appeared black rather than their normal

dark blue in the moonglow. For a second he had the fanciful thought—and he wasn't a man ever given to fanciful thought—that she looked almost otherwordly, as if she was cast of the same stone as her Mercury garden statue. Instinctively he traced a finger over the curve of her cheek. Yes, warm, soft flesh—no cold hard concrete or marble there. It was as if his touch brought her back to life.

"I would be supremely honored to photograph the reunion of five war dogs. But I have one stipulation."

"Name it."

"It's gratis."

That was bullshit. "No. I'm not taking advantage of you. If you do it, then I'm paying you your going rate."

"Mitch, we both know it was my rash action that stuck you with the calendar assignment."

"And your point is?"

"I sort of owe you."

"Baby, you don't owe me anything. From where I'm sitting, this assignment has worked out just fine for me. I'd already checked out who you were and why you were here, but I'm not sure our paths would've crossed again if I hadn't been given the assignment."

"Oh, our paths would've crossed. I had already quizzed Sanchez about you." She made a little moue of disapproval. "You've got to show more initiative Lieutenant Colonel. I had to kiss you. I was prepared to look you up." She shook her head. "You really wouldn't have come looking for me?"

She was teasing but there was a note of seriousness, as well.

Mitch wasn't going to lie to her. It was his modus operandi and regardless she deserved the truth. "No. I wouldn't have."

The truth he didn't voice, however, was the realization that hit him dead in his gut. He wouldn't have gone looking for her because Eden Walters scared the hell out of him.

OUCH, OUCH, AND DOUBLE OUCH. He wouldn't have come looking for her. Well…that wasn't what she'd wanted to hear. She'd asked. She'd pushed. And he'd told her.

She put it in perspective. They'd both known this was a three-day affair…which looked as if it might extend to a five-day affair. And now she was going to meet his grandfather. So, while he wouldn't have come looking for her, well, she'd just have to let that go.

"The assignment sounds really interesting. And it's not as if I have any work scheduled for the weekend, so it's not bumping me out of a project," she said.

"You think it sounds interesting?"

"Of course. It's living history. I've never had an assignment I didn't find interesting. There's merit and value in everything all around us. And for me, I get to capture it. Generations from now someone may l ook at a photo I took and it'll provide an insight, a glimpse of a time that's since passed. It's posterity." Okay, so she'd gotten a little carried away. "And now

I'll climb down off of my soapbox." She tugged the sheet back up.

"I don't mind your soapbox," he said, his voice quiet, reflective. "I never thought of what you do in those terms."

"Lots of people don't." Certainly her parents didn't see it that way. "But that's okay. It's just my take on my career."

"There are two aspects to society. Structure and culture. Without structure, culture can't thrive."

There was no judgment in his voice. He was simply throwing it out his opinion. "And without culture, structure can become oppressive," she countered, her intellect as aroused as her body had been half an hour before. Eden sat up, tucking the sheet around her and Mitch propped himself on the pillow next to her.

And in the moonlit bed, she and Mitch Dugan rambled on about social order, culture, even Sun Tzu's The Art of War—she wasn't sure why he was so surprised she was familiar with the sixth century B.C. Chinese military treatise—until past midnight.

And just because they could agree to disagree on certain points—and agreed on far more points than she would've imagined—that still didn't mean Mitch Dugan was the right man for her. No matter how good he was in bed.

Nope. Three days had become five and then it was over. Even great conversation and even greater sex wasn't going to change that.

10

"THAT'S A WRAP," EDEN SAID and Mitch silently applauded. McElhaney had been part of the final shoot and the sonofabitch had pissed him off to no end. McElhaney had been coming on to Eden all afternoon. She'd ignored what she could and dismissed the rest. A couple of times Mitch had been tempted to intercede but she'd sent him a *back off* glance and Mitch had to respect that she knew what she was doing.

"How about a drink now that we're done with business?" McElhaney persisted.

Sorry, buddy, but she's got plans. We're going to go at it all night long.

"Thanks, but I have another commitment."

"What about afterward?" McElhaney's ego was puncture-proof.

"Let me put this as plain as I know how to put it, Captain McElhaney. I do not want to have dinner, a drink, or even a further conversation with you. I think that should pretty much clear things up for you. Thank you for your time on the calendar."

"You can't just dismiss me like that," McElhaney said, taking a menacing step forward.

Enough was enough. No one talked to Mitch's woman that way. Mitch stepped between McElhaney and Eden. "She just did. I'd suggest you leave now, McElhaney. Assignment over."

Reluctantly, McElhaney backed down and left but not without a sneer at both Mitch and Eden. Mitch had a gut feeling that had he not interceded, McElhaney would've crossed a line and then his ass would've been nailed. But not even for the satisfaction of finally bringing McElhaney down could Mitch allow the asshole to bully Eden.

He turned to her. "I know you were handling it. But he crossed the line and I—"

"It's fine. Really. I appreciate it. You were right about him. He photographs well, but he's certainly obnoxious. I'm not sure he'll make the final cut."

She'd photographed fourteen candidates with the understanding that she'd choose the best dozen and two would be cut. "I can't think of a better guy to dump from the project," Mitch said. "So, this wraps everything up?"

"It's a wrap. I heard from Sergeant Sanchez earlier today, so I need to swing by their place to do the photos I promised."

"I could help you out with that, if you wanted me to. I know my way around the base and Fayetteville, and I'm getting to be a pretty damn good assistant, if I do say so myself."

"A little fine-tuning and I might keep you," she said

with a teasing smile. And then the words lingered between them and seemed to shift and morph into something deeper and more meaningful. She shifted her weight from one foot to another and took a sudden interest in packing away her camera equipment. They both knew there'd be no "keeping" happening on either side.

"THAT'S IT. PERFECT. LAST ONE." Eden snapped off the picture of Sgt. Sanchez with his daughter, Cassie, riding on his shoulders, Liz laughing and holding the toddler in place. "That's definitely a keeper."

Eden couldn't wait to see that shot printed in black and white. "My assistant, Valerie, can send you a disc next week for you to look at and pick your favorites. Or she could e-mail them, if you'd rather."

Mitch stood to the side quietly, watching, seemingly at ease. Eden had the sense that he'd actually enjoyed watching the session with the Sanchez family. She was impressed that for a man used to being in charge, he was equally good at stepping aside and letting her do her own thing. That had certainly never been the case with her parents. Brigadier General Max Walters was always in charge of every situation, whether it was his own or not.

Sanchez laughed. "Seeing as how my wife is the e-mail queen—"

Liz cut him off with an elbow to his side. "E-mail would be great. It saves on postage."

Everyone, even Cassie, laughed as Eden and Mitch moved toward the door. They'd been great subjects to work with because the affection between husband and wife was blatant and their daughter reflected it in spades.

"Thank you again, so much," Liz said, her warm smile enveloping Eden. "I still can't believe you'd make the time to come photograph our family."

"It was my pleasure. And it doesn't begin to compare to what your family has given."

Liz reached out and hugged her, tears shimmering in her eyes. "Thank you. Have a safe trip back to New Orleans. You leave tomorrow?"

"Yep. A bright and early flight. I'll be in touch."

Behind her Mitch and Sanchez exchanged a quick handshake.

"Nice family," Mitch said once they were in his truck, backing out of the driveway.

"Very." She realized that even though she'd been intimate with this man and felt some crazy connection, there was so much about him that she didn't know. At first, she'd thought that was what she wanted but now she realized she'd been wrong. She was already a little in over her head with him, so at this point, why not? She wanted to know more about the man next to her. "Have you ever been married?"

He slanted a look her way that she found impossible to interpret. "Nope. I guess you could say I've committed myself to Uncle Sam. I know there are a lot of people that make it work, but, it's hard on a family. Particularly Special Forces." Covert assignments that meant being incommunicado, heightened danger—it was a tough way for the ones left behind to live.

"So, not even any close calls, huh?"

"What? I'm such a prize you're amazed no one's tried to snap me up?" His grin said he was poking fun at himself, another nice trait in Lieutenant Colonel Dugan.

And yes, that was exactly it. He struck her as the ultimate prize in the Cracker Jack box—not that she had any intention of telling him that. "Don't get carried away."

"What about you? Any ex-husbands lurking in your background?"

"A few," she said with a straight face and then cracked up at his startled expression. "Just kidding. I've been focused on my career, too. I travel a lot and that can make a relationship difficult. On top of that, I've spent a lot of time fixing up my house—it needed a lot of work when I bought it. And there are only so many hours in a day."

"You should've found a handyman—or dated one."

"It was easier to take do-it-yourself classes at Home Depot."

There was a momentary pause and then he laughed. He shook his head. "You do call things the way you see them, don't you?"

"Yeah. I don't see the point in prevarication. I'm

also a lousy strategist. I suck at chess. Heck, I even lose at checkers on a regular basis." She looked over at his chiseled profile and it felt as if her heart skipped a few beats. "I bet you're one heck of a chess player."

He shrugged and there was a hint of nonchalance about it that struck her as odd. He wasn't a particularly nonchalant kind of man.

"Just how good are you at chess? Did you ever win any contests?"

"A couple in high school and later in college."

Hmm. When she had some free time with her laptop she'd be checking that out on Google. But it was obvious he was smart and ambitious. He couldn't be older than his early thirties and he was already a Lieutenant Colonel. Numerous career men retired out at that rank, but Mitch still had a lot of years left. Her own father hadn't made Lieutenant Colonel until much later in his career.

"Your job requires a lot of travel?" he said, following up on her earlier comment. He didn't miss anything.

"My career requires it, but I also like it. I love to discover new places and new experiences. It was the one thing I did like about growing up a military brat."

"But it was the rules you didn't like."

"That and the expectation that my father's career always took precedence over my mother's. Actually, my father's career was my mother's. Her sole purpose in life became only as a useful accessory to him. Don't get me wrong, it's fine for women who want that life-style, but I don't."

"I can't imagine your attitude goes over well with your parents."

"No. It doesn't sit well with Brigadier General and Mrs. Walters." She grinned. "They're really not quite sure where I came from—I'm definitely not the ordinary product of their gene pool and upbringing. What about you? What do your parents think of your career choice?"

Another shrug that spoke volumes with what it didn't say. "I'm not close to my parents. We have different lifestyles and expectations. But I'm close to my grandfather and he's always been supportive."

Of course he was. He was a military man himself. Eden was curious about Mitch's parents. Were they the creative sort, like her, who disliked the rigidity of the military? "Are they artists? Pacifists?"

He laughed again, but this time a margin of bitterness laced his tone. "Um, no. They're pretty much bums. Neither one has ever kept a steady job. They just sort of leeched off of my grandfather for years."

"Oh." There wasn't much to say beyond that. It did explain, however, his devotion to his career…and put him that much further off-limits for anything long-term, not that Eden had ever remotely considered him long-term material. "Will they be at your grandfather's birthday party?"

"It's not likely, unless they think they can get something out of it. I haven't mentioned it and I'm sure the old man hasn't said anything to them. They don't visit him at his assisted-living center, so I seriously doubt it." He offered another shrug and a hard smile. "Of course if they hear there's free food to be had, all bets are off."

Ouch. Note to self. Don't bring up his parents again. It was definitely time for a subject change. "You didn't mention anything about free food. Now I'm definitely sold on the party."

"It's man food. Hot wings, French fries, chili and beer."

"Beer and wings sounds good to me."

"They're going to love you. Just one thing…"

"Yeah?"

"Don't wear the red heels. You don't want to give any of them a heart attack."

"Very funny."

"I'm not kidding. They may be old, but they're men. Those heels might do them in." He winked. "But at least they'll die happy."

11

"THANK YOU FOR FLYING WITH US," the stewardess said as they stepped off of the plane and into the gateway. Mitch was damn glad to get off. He only liked being on planes if he could jump out of them.

Eden shifted her camera bag on her shoulder and switched her carry-on's pull handle to her other hand as they entered the Louis Armstrong New Orleans airport. "I like to travel, but it's always nice to get home." Actually, the high arched ceiling in the main building with its stained glass always did feel a bit like a homecoming.

"Let me take your suitcase," Mitch said.

"I've got it."

"I can put it on top of mine and I won't even know I have it," he said. She was so damn independent but that was one of the things he liked and admired about her. Just one of many, he'd realized last night when they'd checked her out of her hotel and she'd spent her last night in Fayetteville at his house, in his bed. It had been strange—the entire night he'd had a sense of rightness about her being at his house. There'd been no awkwardness, just a completeness, as if he'd found the one thing he hadn't even known he was missing. And how could that be when she couldn't tolerate the one thing, the only thing that defined who and what he was, the military? Mitch didn't doubt her sincerity for a moment. She'd been markedly different every time they'd driven off base.

"Okay, if you can carry it, be my guest."

Mitch made quick work of buckling her suitcase to the top of his.

"Oh, and I get to be on top," she said with a wicked little smile.

The memory of her on top last night came rushing back between them and Mitch felt the familiar spark of arousal that was always a low burn inside him when she was around. She'd liked being on top. He remembered her initial slow ride up and down his shaft. When she'd picked up the momentum, he could barely breathe because he'd been so centered on her slick, tight channel pistoning up and down on him.

He was not going to walk through the airport with a hard-on. He pushed away the thought of her naked, her breasts swaying over him—or at least he tried to. As usual, his discipline suffered a serious set-back with Eden. "Behave, baby."

She looked at him and her eyes challenged his admonition, as if to say, "you know you don't really want me to behave." And no he didn't. He liked the uninhibited way she met him, challenged him, engaged him in the bedroom. Hell, just in general conversation. "At least until we get to your car."

"Fine. I can behave…until we get to my car."

Mitch had cancelled his rental car. He and Eden would drive out to Charoux together for the party. Mitch would see the old man back to the assisted-living center, and they'd return to New Orleans and her house later that night. She'd asked him if he wanted to stay over and see his grandfather again in the morning, but he'd passed. The last thing the old man wanted was Mitch hovering. He liked to stay abreast of Mitch's career and what was going on, but about half a day together every couple of months was all the old man wanted.

She laughed. "I'm driving. You're safe, at least until we get to my house. And then you still get a reprieve because I have a meeting with Valerie, my assistant," she said.

"I looked you up online," he said as they moved through the concourse.

She shot him a swift, surprised look. "You did?"

"Yeah. You've done well for yourself." Her work was featured in several galleries and she ran a small gallery out of her home studio in the French Quarter. Her Mercury photo had been one of the ones featured on her Web page. "I have to say, I don't personally think I look like Mercury but there's something very arresting about the picture."

He wasn't sure how or why, maybe it was part of her

talent coming through, but it seemed to him that the statue was almost lifelike. It left Mitch almost holding his breath waiting to hear what Mercury had to say.

A delighted smile curved her lips. "That's so cool. You got it. I wasn't sure if you would because I work in that realm beyond black and white."

What the hell? He wasn't culturally illiterate, well, not to a severe degree. "I got it. All of your work is like that." It was as if she'd captured the essence, the core of her subjects whether they were living, breathing people or inanimate objects. "I don't pretend to be an expert but it's apparent you have immense talent. I didn't realize how damn lucky the Army was to have you shooting the calendar."

Again, a stillness he'd sensed once or twice before descended on her, even though they were still moving through the airport. It was more a state of being than a state of action. "Thank you."

"I'm looking forward to seeing your gallery."

"You can rummage around while Val and I go over stuff. It won't take long."

"The meeting or the gallery?"

"Both." Her smile was like the sun slipping over the horizon in the morning, dazzling, promising. "Did you want to stay in or go out?"

He had no interest in New Orleans nightlife, but he had plenty of interest in making the most of his remaining time with Eden. "I definitely opt for staying in."

"Good answer. I need to do a little work. I want to

take a look at the calendar shots and the Sanchez family on my good equipment. Val closes the gallery at five and then we'll have the house to ourselves."

The hours before they could be alone felt like a lifetime, but he understood she had business to conduct. "That sounds like a plan."

"Great minds think alike," she quipped.

Actually, considering their differences, he was surprised to find just how much they did think alike on so many issues.

"YOU'RE OFFICIALLY CLOSED FOR business?" Mitch asked from where he stood studying a black-and-white print of a monk on a hilltop at sunset. It was one of her favorites. Traditionally sunsets were captured in vivid color. But when they were done in black-and-white, all the marvelous shades of gray found in the world came through. There was a tranquility about the photo that soothed her soul. Apparently it spoke to Mitch, as well. She'd watched and noted which photos he spent time with.

"Until Monday at noon." Eden closed and locked the front door. She'd lived here three years and never invited a man into her home. Granted plenty of people moved in and out of her gallery, but the rest, the private part, had been just that—private. Sacrosanct.

But it had seemed right to invite Mitch Dugan here. Perhaps because it was as if having Mercury in her garden had already paved the way for Mitch in her private space.

Sleeping with him in a hotel room had been one thing. But then things had shifted when she'd been in his house, in his bed. She knew whatever this was between them was about to change here in her sanctuary, the space she'd created, the home that was an extension of herself. It would now bear the imprint of his presence.

She crossed the gallery floor to the interior French doors covered in heavy drapes that separated the gallery from the rest of the house. They stayed locked during the hours the gallery was open. She unlocked them now.

He was still in front of The Monk, as she thought of the photo. "It's all nice, but I really like this."

She nodded, a glow of pleasure blooming inside. There was nothing quite like having your artistry appreciated. And while "this is nice" from anyone else might seem almost insipid, nothing about Mitch Dugan was hyperbole, so if he said it was nice, it came through as high praise indeed.

"I like that one a lot, as well."

"Why black and white instead of color?"

He was discerning, she'd give him that. "Color is beautiful but the shades of black and white make an impact you simply don't get in the color. It's the juxtaposition of starkness and complexity." He'd either really get it or simply think she was weird.

"It works." He crossed the room slowly, his tread measured, his eyes serious and with each step that he drew closer her heart beat harder and faster until he reached where she stood in the doorway of the French doors leading from her public gallery to her private space. He lightly cupped her shoulders in his hands. "You are a remarkably talented woman, Eden Walters. Your pictures were great on your Web site, but standing here in front of them…Wow."

Emotion washed over her, swamped her, drowned her to the point that tears filled her eyes. Embarrassed by her intense vulnerability, she bowed her head.

"Hey, I didn't mean to upset you."

"No. I'm not upset. I'm just… It's…" She didn't know how to say it because she didn't even know what *it* was, what was going on with her. "It was a very nice thing to say and it moved me."

And then it hit her. She understood precisely why his comment had affected her so. She knew Mitch wasn't exactly like her father, but there were a lot of similarities between them. They were both military men. They both lived and died by structure. And both men were happiest in a world that was black and white.

Her father had always treated her photography as something frivolous. She always had the impression he was waiting for her to grow up and do something important with her life. And yet here was a man with many of the same qualities, only he recognized and lauded her talent.

He smoothed his thumb over her cheek and the tenderness in that simple gesture shook her to her core.

"Show me your house."

"Didn't you look around while I was with Val?"

"Not really." He dipped his head and brushed a butterfly kiss on her lips. "It felt intrusive to look around without you. I'd rather you show me. I'd rather see it through your eyes."

Her heartbeat seemed to echo throughout her body and she paused. Somehow, somewhere this had gone beyond what had started three days ago at Fort Bragg.

"Okay." She caught his hand in hers and led him across the threshold separating the two rooms. "This is the place I call home."

DUSK SETTLED AROUND THEM, filling the corners of the courtyard with shadows. "This place is definitely you," Mitch said from the wrought-iron chair next to hers, the fountain next to them soothing and peaceful. Oddly enough, Mitch felt as comfortable here as he did in his own home in Fayetteville. But was it the place or because *she* was here? "Beautiful, fanciful, orderly but a little bohemian."

"Oh, so you think you've pegged me?" Her ever ready smile lit her face. He brushed aside the thought that he could never get tired of seeing her smile.

He tried to keep it light. "My job is to assess people in a very short period of time so I know what I'm dealing with."

She reached over and traced a faint scar on the back of his hair-smattered hand. "What you're *dealing with?*"

One touch and he was hers. Then again, hadn't it been

that way from the get-go? How could he want her so intensely and still find himself laughing? "That was a general term. Not specific to you." He caught her hand in his and tugged. She obligingly rose and came to him, sinking into his lap. He welcomed the weight of her against his thighs, the intimate press of her buttocks against him, her scent, her warmth, her joy. She wrapped her arms around his neck and her lips unerringly found his.

He slid his hand up to her hip, mapping, memorizing the terrain of her body. "Let's go inside," he murmured against her mouth.

"No. Make love to me here," she said. She leaned back and tugged her shirt over her head. Reaching behind her, her bra followed. In two deft movements the rest of her clothes followed and she stood naked in the semidarkness before him, offering herself.

And he knew, as surely as he knew his own name, that she was offering something special. This wouldn't just be sex on an Indian summer night when the cicadas were still competing with the New Orleans nightlife. She was offering *herself*.

And a stronger man, a better man wouldn't take such a precious gift, but he seemed to have lost himself when it came to her. He stood and silently shed his clothes.

And then in her courtyard he took everything she offered and gave her more than what she'd asked for. But in the end, he wasn't sure that it was an equitable exchange.

12

EDEN MADE A MENTAL NOTE to adjust her camera setting to accommodate the dark paneling, circa the 1960s, that covered the walls of the VFW hall.

"Damn, boy, you found yourself a looker, didn't you?" a bald man with the cane said. Eden thought he'd been introduced as Charlie O'Hannigan.

A man in the wheelchair, sat up a little straighter. "A hooker? She's a hooker? She don't look like a hooker. How much does she cost?"

"Turn up your hearing aid, you old fart," Charlie snapped. "I said looker, not hooker."

She was pretty sure the man in the wheelchair was Jack Phillips. Jack's blue eyes twinkled with mischief. "Oh. Too bad."

Mitch's grandfather snorted. "Too bad my foot. You've been on blood pressure medicine for years. You couldn't get lucky if you wanted to."

"You don't know what the hell you're talking about."

"Damn straight I do."

Eden laughed, thoroughly enjoying the interplay

between the men. Mitch's grandfather still had the erect military carriage that became instinct to most career military men. Mitch bore a striking resemblance to his grandfather, George Lavelle. It was no mystery what Mitch would look like in half a century. The notion gave her a funny feeling in her tummy.

She moved around the room, snapping photographs as the old war dogs positioned themselves at the round table. Jack Phillips was in a wheelchair, having lost his legs to diabetes, according to Mitch. Charlie O'Hannigan walked with a cane. However, the other two men, Tex Rogers and Dickie Turner were still in very good shape considering they were all pushing eighty.

Soon they were drinking beer, gnawing hot wings and meandering into full-blown reminiscing mode. She'd faded into the background which was always her goal in situations such as this.

Mitch had become background, as well. Actually, he was in waiter mode, fetching beer and food refills. She sent a smile his way. "So, how much of being so good to these guys is to be nice, and how much is to monitor their alcohol consumption?"

He grinned, "Busted. About fifty-fifty. The only way Jack's wife would let him come was if I promised her he wouldn't get wasted. Apparently Jack likes to wheelchair race when he's pounded a few too many. He's always been the cutter in the group."

Eden smiled. Every once in a while, Mitch's Southern boy upbringing came through. She found it charming.

"Your grandfather's the leader, isn't he?"

Mitch nodded. "He was their ranking NCO. The old man never talks about it, but the other guys love to tell how he saved their butts when he roused them all to move out in the middle of the night. They found out the next day the Chinese were right across the Yalu River."

"Korea?"

"Yeah."

"He's got that same air of authority you have."

"We're a lot alike. These guys were always my heroes growing up. It's men like them who made our country what it is today. I hope one day I'll be sitting here, listening to my grandson say the same thing about me."

Eden had an instant snapshot of Mitch's grandson-to-be appear in her head. She saw a striking replica of Mitch…only with her coloring. A shiver ran through her. That was definitely dangerous territory to wander into. He shifted and she realized he'd just revealed perhaps more than he'd meant to.

"I have no doubt your grandson will be saying exactly that one day," she said softly.

His gaze snared hers and she could swear he was seeing the same possible grandson. Her heart tripped against her ribs. Mitch looked away first and Eden struggled to regain her composure. This never happened to her.

She trained her camera back on the group and fired

off a shot. That'd be a wash. Her hand had been unsteady and blurred photos didn't work.

Mitch replenished the hot wings and joined the men, settling back in his chair and stretching his legs out before him. He didn't join in the conversation but took a long pull of his own beer and seemed to thoroughly enjoy the tall tales being swapped.

Watching through the lens, she saw the looks that passed between him and his grandfather. Affection. Respect. Understanding. A shared love of service to country and fellow man. Click. Click. Click. And she knew. That was the good stuff she wanted. Needed. And then she narrowed the focus of the lens until it was all Mitch, only Mitch.

In the instant, in the moment she snapped his picture, her heart echoed the same click. It wasn't so much a conscious thought as it was a total state of being. She loved him. Loved the strong line of his jaw and the masculine yet tender regard he had for his grandfather. And fast on the heels of her realization came the absolute certainty that the two of them had no future.

She didn't belong in Mitch Dugan's world. And Mitch Dugan's world was everything to him.

"I LIKE HER," the old man said as Mitch walked up the sidewalk leading from the parking lot to the assisted-living center beside him. Eden had insisted on staying in the car and catching up on phone calls. Mitch was certain, however, that she was simply giving him and the old man time alone.

His grandfather leveled a frank look his way. "You need to hang on to her."

"I just met her four days ago."

"I saw your grandmother across the room and I knew. She'd come to a dance with her cousin Edna. I was married to that woman fifty-eight and a half years." The old man never failed to include that half year. "I saw the way you looked at this girl. Nothing wrong with my eyesight now that I've had those cataracts removed. Don't tell me you don't know, too."

Mitch opened his mouth to deny it and realized he couldn't. He simply didn't know. He was used to black and white. Cut and dried. He was used to making a quick assessment, a decision, and living with that. However, Eden wasn't so easily pegged. Plain and simple, Mitch was confused. It was a struggle, hell it was downright painful to admit it to the old man, but he did.

"I don't know."

Another one of those laser looks from the old man. "All right then. But you better not take too long to figure it out cause gals like that don't come your way every day."

They entered the front door and headed down the hall.

"I've never met anyone like her before."

"That's what I'm talking about. Where's that ability to make snap decisions that made you a Lieutenant Colonel at thirty?"

The old man was proud as hell of that. Mitch was frank with his grandfather in a way he wasn't with anyone else. But then again, no one else would've dared pose that question to him. "It seems to have deserted me."

A sly humor glinted in the old man's eyes. "Boy, if that doesn't tell you what you need to know…. Are you waiting for someone to hit you over the head with a brick?" He unlocked his room door and Mitch followed him into the apartment that held a fraction of the furniture and mementos that had made George and Cherie Lavelle's house on Winnow Street in Charoux a home.

The old man retreated to his recliner and Mitch took a spot on the love seat next to it. Then he gave the old man the whole story. He briefed him on Eden, her father, her background, her reaction to the military. "And I saw her house and studio in New Orleans. You've never seen a person more where they belong than she did there. And she's so damned talented it's scary."

Now his grandfather would understand. Now he'd tell Mitch the only logical course of action was for her to go her way and Mitch to go his.

"If you want something bad enough, you figure out how to make it happen. The problem isn't in the situation. The problem is in how bad you want it." He offered a sharp nod, dismissing the matter, having spoken his piece. "You did good with that get-together, boy." The subject change was the old man's way of telling Mitch that the topic of Eden was closed…for now. "The beer was cold, the wings were hot, and Jack's old lady can't complain." The old man snorted. "Well, she can and she will, but that's just the way she is."

"Glad you had a good time."

"If I don't kick the bucket in the next twelve months I'd like to do it again."

"How about six months?"

"Scared to push it, boy?"

"Can't see the downside to it."

"This had to set you back a pretty penny."

He'd covered the costs of flying in the other guys and their wives and putting them up at the local motel. It'd been worth every red cent. "It didn't break my bank."

"Then we'll see if Jack's old lady will let him out to play again in six months' time. Now I need to rest and you need to get back to that gal of yours."

Mitch had to say it was a good feeling to know Eden was waiting out for him in the parking lot. Not just for the sex he knew was coming but for the conversation. He was eager to hear her take on the evening.

"I'll be in touch."

"I know you will."

The old man stopped him as he opened the door leading to the hall. "Boy…"

Mitch turned. "Sir?"

"Don't let her get away."

"Ten-four."

What the old man didn't understand was that not letting her get away would destroy her.

13

A FEW HOURS LATER, THEY SAT in Eden's parlor, sharing the sofa. But the intimacy of the last few days had disappeared. Mitch had been reserved, distant on the drive back home. She'd reminded herself all the way back to New Orleans that this had been inevitable. Still, it didn't make it any easier. And she didn't understand why he'd suddenly built a wall between them.

"Thanks again for coming along today," he said. "Your assistant will send them along with a bill?"

"We're not having the bill discussion," she said, her throat growing tight with what felt like, correction, what *was* goodbye. "It was an honor to be there."

"The guys certainly enjoyed you being there. They may be old but a man never gets tired of looking at a beautiful woman."

She opened her mouth to correct him. She wasn't beautiful. She dressed to her strengths and aimed to look her best but…. Then again, Mitch Dugan wasn't a man with a glib tongue. If he wanted to tell her she was beautiful, by God she'd take that.

"Thank you. Mitch…" She paused. She'd never told

a man she loved him before—well, her junior high crush didn't count and this was nothing like the puppy love she'd had for Rodney Metcalf at fourteen. Maybe it wasn't the wisest decision she'd ever made, but it seemed wrong to feel this way about someone and not tell them. In her book, love and joy were meant to be shared, even if they weren't reciprocated. And it wasn't as if she'd taken the safe, wise route with him from day one, had she?

"Yes?" he prompted but she didn't miss the guarded note in his voice.

"I wanted you to know…" She stopped and tried again. "Do you come back often to visit your grandfather?"

"Seldom. Usually once or twice a year. He said if he hasn't kicked the bucket—his terminology, not mine—in six months he wants another reunion."

She nodded. "You're welcome to stop over."

His eyes were as unfathomable as those of her courtyard statue. "That could get awkward, couldn't it?"

"How so?"

"What if you were involved with someone else?"

"What if I wasn't?"

"There's no reason to think you wouldn't be."

How did she tell a man she'd only met days ago that she'd fallen head over heels in love with him without coming across as some needy stalker chick? Especially since he wasn't exactly coming across as being interested in moving forward. But how did she walk away from what she felt for him, what she felt between them, without trying?

"Yes, there is. There's every reason. All you have to do is ask me."

"I don't have that right. I live in North Carolina. Near an Army base. You know what that means."

Yes, she knew. It meant limited leave time. Limited time of his own in general. It meant all the rules she'd been so happy to escape from as an adult. But she felt they could find a way to work through it, if only he could see things as something other than black and white.

She took a deep breath and leaped off the edge of the cliff. "It's funny how life has a way of handing us exactly what we think we don't want. Maybe that's what I want."

Mitch shook his head slowly and his gaze swept the room. "This is where you belong. Just like the Army is where I belong. We both know they're worlds apart."

"Does it matter anywhere in your assessment of our situation that I love you?"

There was a flicker of joy, of acknowledgement in his eyes which he quickly banked. But she had seen it, felt it. Whatever came out of his mouth, he loved her, too. "It doesn't change the outcome."

It didn't surprise her, but it hurt nonetheless. "There are some people who have jobs that they get up and go to and at the end of the day, they're done. We both know that's not us. What we do is who we are."

She did love him as surely as the sun would rise in the East in the morning and set in the western sky. An offer hovered on the tip of her tongue—to move to North Carolina, to Fayetteville and become part of his world. A cold sweat broke out over her skin. She couldn't do it. Couldn't say it. She was where she belonged, as was Mitch.

Tomorrow he would leave. Tomorrow she'd only have memories of the last few days and nights. Tomorrow and all the days that would follow, she could mourn what couldn't be. But tonight she would spend making memories.

Eden linked her arms around his neck and kissed him, loving him enough to let him go, hoping her actions spoke louder than words.

TWO WEEKS LATER MITCH SAT at his desk and opened the overnight packet. The old man's reunion photos. Only the photos weren't the first thing he looked at. He picked up the sheet of paper on top. Eden had included a brief note, telling him she hoped he was pleased with the photos and asking if all was well with him. He could swear he caught a whiff of her scent from the paper.

"What you got there, Lieutenant Colonel?" Murdoch asked, dropping into the chair opposite Mitch's desk.

"Pictures from the geezer get together."

"How'd they turn-out?"

He was in a piss-poor mood. The only upside to

being back at work was that he'd learned that McEl-haney had finally pissed off the wrong person and was now facing a disciplinary hearing. Still, it didn't give him the satisfaction he expected to feel. He looked back at the photos. "I just opened them, Murdoch."

Murdoch, however, remained unfazed by his abruptness. "Well then, let's see."

At the bottom of the packet, was a bubble-wrapped package with a sticky note on top. *For your desk.* Mitch opened it. A simple, stark black frame held a candid shot of all of them sitting around the table. But it was more than that. It was as if, for that moment in time, she'd captured the history, the shared experiences, the brotherhood that bound the five men.

"Damn, that's nice."

"It is, isn't it?" Mitch thumbed through the photos. He'd really look at them later. "She does good work."

"You talked to her?"

"No."

"You haven't called her?"

"I'm busy. She's busy. She's got her career. I've got mine. It was never meant to be anything more."

He said aloud what he'd told himself over and over since he'd returned from New Orleans. He should've come back to Bragg and stepped back into his job, picked up his life. Only it hadn't happened that way. Mitch, the man who'd always had spectacularly singular focus, couldn't get Eden Walters out of his head.

Murdoch grew uncharacteristically somber. "I wasted a couple of years and damn near walked away from the best thing that ever happened to me. Eden scares the hell out of you, doesn't she?"

There was no room for fear in Mitch's life. He'd been trained to set a desired outcome and move forward on that mission. But as much as he wanted to tell Murdoch it was none of his damn business, much as he wanted to deny it, Mitch wasn't a coward. "Yes. She scares the hell out of me."

"That's because she's your weak spot. There's no armor in the world that can protect you against her. And the sad news, buddy, is that it's not going to change, no matter how damn hard you try to deny it. You're done for. Been there. Done that. Got the badge…and the ring. Don't sit around and lose the best thing that ever happened to you." Murdoch pushed to his feet. "I'm outta here. Tara's dragging me to a movie."

"Close the door on your way out."

Mitch sat at his desk and it was as if a mortar shell had just landed next to him. He felt shattered. Disoriented. Damn Murdoch to hell and back. He loved Eden. Walking away from her hadn't changed a damn thing. He still loved her. Ignoring the old man's advice hadn't mattered a hill of beans. He still loved her. And he always would. Yeah, she was his weak spot, his Achilles' heel and that might be uncomfortable as hell, but it was what it was.

So, he loved her and she loved him. But how the hell

did they make this work? The framed photo on his desk caught his eye. She'd printed it in black and white but he realized that it was all the shades of gray on the glossy paper, all the in-betweens that gave it the depth and the meaning she'd captured with the lens.

Their future, their relationship didn't have to be black and white. Maybe it was in exploring the shades of gray that they'd find a way to make things work. She'd asked him once if he would have came looking for her and he'd said no. That was about to change.

He'd accrued plenty of leave time over the past few years. He just needed a favor or two to get it pushed through pronto. He picked up the phone.

He had to get back to New Orleans. And Eden.

14

"THE CALENDAR PROOFS are ready for approval," Val said, standing in the door of Eden's office. "I'm overnighting them today. That gives the base commander a month to review them."

Eden made a snap decision. "Cancel the FedEx. I'll deliver them." Enough was enough. She'd waited and waited and waited…and been absolutely miserable. If Mitch really didn't want her, didn't want to find a way to make them work, then let him say so. She'd replayed that last night in her head a thousand times. He hadn't told her he loved her, but he hadn't told her he didn't, either. And what made her so good at her craft was her ability to read people. It wasn't desperation or some crazy infatuation on her part—Mitch Dugan loved her. It was in his eyes, in his kiss, in the tender way he'd made love to her in her courtyard.

She'd sought solace in her work, her home, her life and all she'd found was that whatever she'd had before, whatever used to be enough for her, wasn't near enough now. Not without him.

Val's eyebrows shot up to her hairline. "You're going to deliver them to the FedEx office? Why do that when they pick up here at the door?"

Feeling better than she had since Mitch Dugan had walked out of her life, Eden smiled at her confused assistant. "No. I'm delivering them to Fort Bragg. Can you book me a flight for tomorrow morning?"

A sly, knowing smile spread over Val's face. "Ah. I see. Rental car? Return flight?"

"Rental car and just go with an open-ended ticket. What do I have scheduled for next week?"

"You're in Boston Thursday and Friday but it could be rescheduled without a lot of hassle."

"I'll let you know."

Eden felt a surge of panic and excitement. If she was going to Fort Bragg tomorrow, she had a lot to do today. She needed a haircut. Her nails. A wax job. If she was laying siege to Lieutenant Colonel Mitch Dugan, she was going in armed to the teeth.

MITCH GOT IN HIS BRONCO. Suitcase? Check. Cell phone? Check. Airline ticket? Che— Dammit to hell. He'd left it on his desk.

He climbed out of the truck and headed back into the building, pronto. He'd been ready to leave when Hardwick had requested some last-minute bullshit paperwork and then he'd been in such a damn hurry, he'd left the ticket on the corner of his desk. Just the kind of thing he never did, but he was coming to realize that when it came to matters involving Eden, his norm went out the window.

Traffic would be a bitch on a Friday afternoon and if he missed his flight… He rounded the corner and collided with another moving object. In a moment of extreme déjà vu, he found Eden sprawled at his feet in that pencil skirt and those sexy red heels. Or maybe he'd just slipped over the edge. He shook his head to clear it, but she was still there. He realized he was grinning like an idiot.

"We've got to stop meeting like this," he said, saying the only thing he could think of. Damn. Now he not only looked like an idiot, he sounded like an idiot.

"I don't know, soldier, I'm pretty okay with meeting like this. You know what's going to happen when you help me up, don't you, Lieutenant Colonel?"

Not just no, but hell no. No more public kisses in the hallway.

"We'll take that up in my office, Ms. Walters."

Mercifully his office was the second door on the left. Before she could blink properly he had her on her feet, in his office and against the closed door. Then his mouth was on her—her lips, her neck, her shoulder. His fingers were in her hair and he wanted to absorb her into himself. It was that same rush he felt when he jumped, ripped the chord and engaged his chute, only better. A thousand times better.

"I was an idiot," he said, in between kisses.

"You won't get any argument from me."

"A token protest would've been nice."

"Sorry." Ha! She was totally unrepentant. That was, however, one of the very things he loved about her. And speaking of…. "I love you."

"I know."

"You do?"

"Of course. But it's nice to hear you say it. It's about time you manned up."

"Manned up?" He laughed. She'd never let him get the upper hand, at least not for long. And she was exactly what he wanted, what he needed. He sobered. "I love you, baby, but how are we going to make this work? I've turned this over a million times in my head. I can't ask you to move here and I can't give up the military. How do we make it work?"

He was turning it over to her. He was used to being in charge, calling the shots, but in this…he needed her insight, her unique way of viewing the world. His world. Her world. Hopefully, *their* world.

"It's unorthodox. It's different. And it'll mean compromise."

"I'm listening."

"We split our time between New Orleans and wherever you're stationed. We won't always be together."

"You mean six months on, six months off?"

"There you go with a schedule," she said with a teasing smile. "No, not exactly. You can make up a schedule if you want to, but it isn't necessary. Basically, you'll spend part of your leave in New Orleans and I'll spend part of my non-travel time where you are. Like I said, we won't always be together, but I'll always be waiting for you, whether it's here or there."

Mitch took a minute to wrap his head around the notion. Military relationships...what the hell, who was he kidding, military marriages were unorthodox to begin with. There was a lot of time spent away from family. The only difference would be that she wouldn't be cooling her heels in Fayetteville when he was away on assignment. "As long as you're mine at the end of the day, I can't see that anything else matters."

Tears gathered in her eyes and clung to her lashes.

"Hey, that was supposed to be good news."

She sniffled. "It is, you idiot."

"I was coming for you," he said.

"You were?"

"I was." He moved away from her arms long enough to snag his airline ticket from his desk. "I didn't have a plan, I didn't have the answer, but I was coming for you, baby."

"Oh, Mitch," she said, melting against him, into him.

Once again, he felt that ripped sensation, only this time, he knew that a safe landing was only the beginning. He never, ever wanted to free-fall without her being there to catch him, to save him from the impact.

"I need you. I love you. Marry me."

"Is that an order, Lieutenant Colonel?"

Her tone was playful but he sensed the deeper side

to her question. She needed to know their marriage wouldn't be like the one her parents had, that he wouldn't require her to subjugate her career—or herself—to him. "No, baby. There won't be any orders issued between us." Then remembering the games they played in the bedroom, he added, "Unless you want me to, of course."

"Roger that, soldier."

* * * * *

Wait!
Now that Mitch and Eden have finally
decided to make a go of it, aren't you
wondering how Eli Murdoch and his wife,
Tara, ended up so blissfully—and dare I say it,
sickeningly—happy?
Find out in our bonus read,
TRIPLE THREAT,
by Jennifer LaBrecque.
Enjoy!

Triple Threat

1

"WHERE ARE YOU HEADED?" Captain Eli Murdoch asked, his duffel bag slung over his shoulder as he and another soldier crossed the parking lot at Fort Benning, Georgia, home of the U.S. Army's paratrooper jump school.

"Anywhere but this hellhole," Lieutenant Colonel Mitch Dugan said with a grin.

Mitch was full of shit. Eli and Mitch had met five years ago in basic training, fresh out of college, both ROTC guys, and struck up a friendship. After spending the last five years at different bases, they'd both made the decision to move into Special Forces and wound up at the same three-week jump school rotation.

Eli had embraced every minute of the challenge that was paratrooper training. Mitch hadn't been one to shy away from the challenges, either.

"So, your folks already headed down to Florida?" Mitch said.

"Yeah, they drove down from Tennessee a couple of days ago so they could be here this morning, but they're back on the road now. They'll spend a week with my sister and her triplets. Better them than me. Teresa's kids are cute but they're wild. Seriously, man, they could bring those hellions in for Special Ops training and they'd probably kick our asses."

This morning, after three weeks of intense training, Eli and Mitch had earned their wings and become part of an elite fraternity, the Airborne. Eli's folks had shown up at 0900 at the south end of Eubank Field on Airborne Walk to observe the final jumps, the graduation ceremony and the awarding of the coveted paratrooper wings. And then they'd promptly continued south.

His mother's eyes had sparkled with unshed tears and a quiet pride when she'd hugged him. "Grandpa would be so proud of you. In fact, I think he's watching and he's proud right now," she'd whispered.

Funny, but Eli had felt the same way—that the grandfather who'd regaled him with tales of serving on the European front in World War II and later in Korea and Vietnam was aware that today his grandson had taken one step closer to being a more effective soldier. A paratrooper. From the time he was a kid, Eli had known he was meant to serve and defend his country.

Not surprisingly, no one had shown up on Mitch's behalf. From what Eli had seen over the years they'd been Regular Army together, Mitch's family was a bunch of losers. Eli knew he was blessed with a close-knit, albeit small, family. No matter how far across the globe he was stationed, he always knew his folks and his buddies who'd stayed in Jackson Flats, Tennessee, had his back. He'd always had a home base. Mitch, on the other hand, never elected to visit family on leave. Not once, ever. The guy was straight discipline, hardcore army all the way. Eli had invited Mitch to come home with him a couple of times for the holidays, but it soon became apparent that even though they were friends, Mitch wasn't going to take him up on his offer.

Mitch laughed now at Eli's assessment of his three nephews. "Mini-terrorists, eh?"

"You don't even want to know," Eli said. *Hellion* was a good term for them. His mother said they reminded her of him at that age. He grinned. "Are you taking leave?"

"Nope. I'm heading up to Bragg." That didn't surprise Eli, either. Special Forces training would continue at Fort Bragg, home of the 82nd Airborne and Special Operations Forces in North Carolina. There they'd become the crème de la crème—some of the most valuable soldiers in the military, Special Forces officers, experts in unilateral direct action operations and unconventional warfare. Eli had an affinity for languages. The weeks prior to jump school he'd completed an intense course in Farsi.

"Where are you heading?" Mitch asked.

"Back home for the weekend. Another one of my buddies is getting married. Poor bastard. I'll stay at my folks' place, even though they're away right now." His friends were dropping like flies now. This was number four. And Eli had agreed to be a groomsman when said bastard, Greg Waddell, married Lisa Mosley. He and Greg had had a reputation in town for pulling some harmless but dumb-ass pranks when they were younger, like spray painting the town water tower one night. Eli had the leave time coming and it'd be cool to reconnect with some of the people from his severely misspent youth. It was kind of strange that while he'd spent the last several years traveling the globe, so many of the people he'd grown up with had stayed in Jackson Flats.

And *she* would be there. His gut clenched at the thought of Tara Swenson…her mouth, her hands, her soft, soft skin, her legs wrapped around his waist, her writhing beneath him, on top of him… This time he was definitely staying away. Twice had been two times too many. No more close encounters of the hot kind with her.

"You need a psych eval, man, if you're spending your leave at some wedding."

Eli shrugged, stopping at his pride and joy, his 2008 Shelby Mustang GT500KR, black with silver stripes and packing 500 horses in the engine. He popped the trunk. "They're not bad and the parties afterward are usually kick-ass." *That* was an understatement.

His first buddy had succumbed to matrimony five years ago. Eli had been fresh out of college and had just been handed down his commission. Yeah, he'd thought he was the man. The champagne had been endless and the night had been hot. And what had started out as a casual romp had turned into something way, way more…so *not* what he wanted, needed or was looking for. He'd woken up the next morning, looked into Tara's sea-green eyes and felt something inside him turn upside down.

And in keeping with his military strategic training, he'd taken the only viable course of action. Far better that a soldier retreat than surrender. So, he'd run like hell in the other direction.

And then, there was Christy and Matt's wedding two years ago. Hell, they'd divorced before the ink was dry on the license. But Tara had been there. Neither one of them had planned to hook up, but dammit to hell he couldn't keep his hands off her. Before the night was over, they were wearing out the sheets in a hotel thirty miles away.

His entire body tightened, quickened when he remembered the hottest sex he'd ever had. He'd almost called her after that night. Hell, he'd even put together an e-mail once and then deleted it. He was heading overseas and that didn't make him much of a candidate for a relationship. It wasn't fair to her. And besides, his career plans didn't include any emotional commitments. He suspected Tara was the one woman who could derail those plans. So, they'd scorched the bed…and the carpet…and the shower… And, once again, he'd walked away.

He shook his head, trying to dislodge the memories.

Then he put his duffel bag in the trunk and slammed it closed.

Mitch frowned. "I tell you what. I'll stick with the bar scene and leave the wedding deals to you."

"How 'bout you recon the bars up at Bragg before I get there?"

Mitch strode over to his restored-to-mint-condition '69 Ford Bronco. "Deal. Enjoy your wedding."

"Will do." He planned to have a helluva good time. And he was due a little R&R after busting his balls for his wings the last three weeks. After all, there were lots of fish in the sea. And this time, he'd make it a point to fish far, far away from where he might catch Tara.

Because come hell or high water, he was not sleeping with Tara Swenson again.

2

"ELI'S FLYING IN this afternoon. Greg's picking him up at the airport and they're heading straight to the rehearsal," Lisa Mosley said as she strolled into Tara's now-empty classroom after a cursory knock.

Tara knew he was coming, that he was one of the groomsmen, but hearing Lisa say it, sent her stomach somersaulting. Tara was a bridesmaid. She'd be at the rehearsal. He'd be at the rehearsal. The situation had disaster written all over it. But then, she'd known Eli had disaster written all over him from the first minute she'd seen him in high school and felt her heart drop into her stomach…and he hadn't seen her at all.

She glanced up from the pile of essays her eighth graders had turned in last period. Despite the upheaval inside her, she strove for calm nonchalance. "And I care, why?"

Lisa settled on the edge of Tara's desk. "Hel-lo. I distinctly remember what happened two years ago when Christy and Matt got married."

Good Lord, Lisa would be insufferable if she only knew that it had been the second time Tara had slept with

Eli. In a moment of weakness, she'd confessed that second indiscretion to Lisa, but thank God, had the good sense to not tell her it was bedroom romp numero dos. "Everyone's allowed one mistake—" or two "—in a lifetime."

Lisa stared her down, continuing her interrogation Spanish Inquisition–style. "Are you bringing a date to the wedding?"

Tara abandoned the essays. Grading them wasn't going to happen today. She leaned back in her chair, crossed her arms and returned Lisa's stare. "I don't need to bring a date to the wedding. I'm an independent woman who doesn't have to have a man attached to her side to prove anything, thank you."

"Anthony was busy?"

Smirking really wasn't attractive on Lisa, but Tara held her tongue.

"Well, yeah." Okay, so Tara *had* known a moment of last-minute panic. True enough, she didn't need a man, but having a human shield between her and Captain Hard Body had suddenly struck her as a prudent move.

Eli Murdoch was her Achilles' heel. Her weak spot. If she could keep him at arm's length then he couldn't get close enough to get around her. She just didn't think she could put herself through another great-sex-and-then-he-never-calls episode again.

Hence, she'd made an emergency plea to Anthony Caldwell, who was nothing more than a friend and totally, blindly in love with Trish McGee, who'd stupidly moved in with the good-for-nothing Mac Taylor—the intricacies of small-town relationships could be mind-boggling. But Anthony was out of town on business.

Which meant that Tara had to face Eli Murdoch on her own.

"Eli's going to be your escort." Lisa shot her an arch look.

"I wish you hadn't…"

"Where there are sparks, there's fire. Look at me and Greg. We're the last two people you'd expect to get married."

Wasn't that the truth? Lisa was the smart chick with the smart mouth and Greg was your typical Tennessee good ol' boy—but what they had worked. Still, Lisa, who always thought she knew best, was wasting her time having Eli escort Tara. *Whatever.*

"I think I can handle hooking my arm through his without throwing him to the church floor and having my wicked way with him."

"Are you sure about that?"

Actually, she wasn't altogether certain—but she was darn sure going to try. For some crazy, totally frightening reason, all of her self-control seemed to desert her whenever she was close to his dark-haired, dark-eyed, chiseled-lipped, breathtakingly broad-shouldered, hard-bodied six-foot-two self.

Willpower? Gone.

Common decency? Out the window.

She remembered every inch, every nuance of him in excruciating, maddening detail even though it had been two years. The way his fingers had curled through hers when he held her hands above her head, against the smooth cotton sheets…the low, guttural sound he made in the back of his throat when she traced her finger along the muscled ridge bisecting his hip.

"It shouldn't be a problem," Tara said.

"You do realize that if Eli wasn't a problem for you, you wouldn't have had to turn to Anthony as a stand-in date? You'd have a real date."

Now Lisa was just getting ridiculous. As if Eli Murdoch had any bearing on her love life or immediate lack thereof. "Please. I've dated guys. I just happen to be in between."

She'd had two lovers since the last time she'd slept with Eli. One guy a year didn't seem excessive. They'd been competent, and one would think that one man's warm breath against her neck would feel the same as another's, that the rasp of male stubble against her bare skin shouldn't vary much from man to man. But it did. Neither of her subsequent lovers had come close to measuring up to Eli—literally or figuratively.

Unfortunately, Eli was the wrong man for her. She'd always known it—from the very first moment she'd laid eyes on him when she'd transferred to Jackson Flats High School as a sophomore. Her breath caught in her throat as she recalled the very instant she'd seen him, a senior, decked out in his ROTC uniform, so commanding with his broad shoulders and height, so compelling with his piercing dark eyes, so handsome, it was as if everything inside her melted.

He'd clearly been eager to shake the dust of Jackson Flats from his heels and embark on a military career that meant moving often. She'd just arrived, desperate to settle into one place and call it home, after being dragged over the great state of Tennessee by her mother since the time she was a small child. Tara craved stability, she needed to put down roots.

"Well, I'm betting you wind up back in the sack with him this time, too."

Falling into bed with Eli, yet again—and at a damn wedding once again—wasn't going to happen. She hadn't heard a single word from him in two years—no phone call, no e-mail, no message via friends. God, she'd have to be flat-out stupid or desperate—and she was neither.

"I'll walk down the aisle with him—" Whoa, that came out all wrong. "—in your wedding, but that's it. Nothing else. Not even a kiss."

Ohmigod. Why'd she mention a kiss? The man kissed like heaven—regardless of where or what he was kissing. White-hot heat flashed through her.

Lisa shot her a knowing look. "Uh-huh."

Tara ignored the clamor of certain body parts that

were already waving a white flag of surrender in anticipation. "Absolutely. And I'll make sure he knows it right up front."

3

ELI LEFT HIS DUFFEL BAG in the trunk of Greg's ride and sauntered toward the First Methodist Church of Jackson Flats. A brisk wind whistled through February's bare branches.

"Lisa was all nervous that we'd be late and here we are with—" Greg checked his wristwatch "—three minutes to spare. I've still got time to get in a smoke."

Eli laughed, pushing his buddy toward the front steps of the steepled, stained glass building. "You need to give that up, man. It's gonna kill you. And if you're late, Lisa's gonna kill me. Keep walking."

Greg shot him a pitiful glance that didn't even begin to disguise the sudden onset of "oh-shit-I'm-about-to-give-up-my-freedom" jitters. "You're whipped and she's not even your fiancée."

"Nuh-uh. There's a difference between being smart and being whipped. You've got about eighteen hours left to figure it out."

Eli climbed the first step and his heart slammed against his ribs. Damn but he needed to get a handle on himself. He'd recently completed a number of night jumps and managed to stay calm, cool and collected. So how had one woman managed to tie him up like this? He had to get a grip. It was all the more reason not to do something stupid like hook up again. No…not, just no, hell no.

Greg had filled him in on the other members of the bridal party. Traci Rowell, one of the bridesmaids, had always been cute and as far as he knew, was still unattached. Tara wasn't the only game in town. He'd send a clear concise message he wasn't interested this time.

Then suddenly, it was showtime. Greg pushed open one of the front double doors and announced in his booming voice, "Look who I found loitering at the airport."

There was a sudden pause in conversation and then everyone headed toward them, pretty much all talking at once. Part of Eli's training included making snap situation assessments. He noted everyone in the wedding party, but his gaze immediately sliced through the crowd to Tara, like a laser locking onto a target.

Some women didn't age well. Unfortunately, she wasn't one of them. She looked even better than he remembered, and he'd remembered her looking pretty damn good. Her honey-blond hair that had been cut in a chin-length bob two years ago, now hung past her shoulders…long enough to brush against his skin if she leaned over him… A new pair of square-shaped glasses framed her green eyes—very sexy. Her mouth, however, had remained unchanged—wide, generous, tempting. And the lush curves of her body he'd so enjoyed were still enough to send his pulse into over-drive.

Lisa, Greg's outspoken bride-to-be, launched herself at Eli, enveloping him in a sisterly hug. "Hey, you. You're a sight for sore eyes."

And then the rest of his old schoolmates greeted him, exchanging hellos and handshakes. He didn't miss the fact, however, that Tara held herself apart, even though he could feel the heat of her green eyes scanning him from head to toe, covering all the interesting spots in between.

After a few minutes, Mrs. Cantrell, the wedding director, took over. "Okay, since we're all here now, let's get started. First, I'm going to pair up the grooms-men and bridesmaids so you know how to line up and who'll be escorting whom out. Just move to the side when I call your names." She glanced down at her notepad and began to read off her list. Third pair down she announced, "Eli Murdoch, Tara Swenson."

As they moved to the side, Eli whispered, "Hi, Tara." He was in imminent danger of drowning in her sea-green eyes.

"Hello, Eli." She tucked her hair behind one pink-shelled, double-pierced ear. Dammit, even her ears were sexy. He remembered nibbling at that delicate little lobe, and Tara making the softest moan in the back of her throat… "Stop it," she hissed under her breath.

"What?" He hadn't done anything. He hadn't even touched her. Still, her scent wrapped around him, evoking the memory of her smell on his skin after sex, her taste against his tongue.

"Quit looking at me like that." Her eyes were taking on that smoky, glazed look he knew so intimately.

"Like what?"

"You know what."

"I wouldn't ask if I knew, would I?"

She turned her head away from the rest of the wedding party and said in a low voice that cut right through him, "Don't look at me like you'd like to eat me up."

Okay, so maybe he *had* checked her out when he came in. Last time he noticed, he was still a red-blooded American male, but what the hell. She'd given him the once-over, too. "Well, then maybe you shouldn't look at me that way."

"You wish." She crossed her arms over her chest and shot him a smoldering look that didn't do a damn thing to bank the fire she'd started inside him. Because, quite frankly, her actions just showcased her well-rounded assets. "And just for the record, I'm telling you up front, I'm not going to—" she lowered her voice to a husky almost-whisper "—make the same mistake I've made at the last two weddings."

Exactly his thought. They were on the same page. "I'm glad to hear it."

"You are?" She looked...shocked. She quickly recovered her aplomb. "Well, of course you are. We're both using better judgment this time."

"Yep. You'll be relieved to know I'm not planning to…follow that path, either."

"That's…great," she said, her smile overly bright, a tad strained. "It's a big relief."

"Glad we got that out of the way."

"Yep."

"Okay, everyone." Mrs. Cantrell clapped her hands together. "Ladies, if you'll move to the rear of the church. Gentleman, I'd like you to gather at the front pew."

"She said gentlemen, but I bet she wants you up there, too," Tara said with a sassy smirk before heading to the back of the church.

He stood momentarily transfixed by the bounce of her blond hair against her shoulders and the sensual sway of her hips as she took a shortcut through the pews.

Good thing they'd cleared the air. Because right now, he wanted desperately to kiss the top of her head and her feet and every space in between.

4

"LET'S TRY THIS AGAIN. We've got to get things right before we can finish up," Mrs. Cantrell intoned from the front of the church.

"Again?" Tara said, her stomach bottoming out.

How long would they spend going through the exit routine? This was the third time Kathy Farland had missed her cue. Which meant it was the third time Tara had to link her arm through Eli's.

She knew it shouldn't be a big deal. The problem was, she couldn't link her arm though his without feeling the play of all those hard muscles, getting caught up in the incendiary heat that seemed to roll off of him, surrounding her with his scent, his heat, him. It was a rapid plunge into lust-driven madness. Two lousy, long years and simply standing next to him made her body hum.

Again? Was he remembering, too?

His eyes, so dark when he was aroused it was difficult to tell where his pupils began and ended, snared hers. The slow slide of a smile across his well-shaped mouth held a feral edge. "Again."

God, yes, he remembered. The last time. She'd still been riding the final wave of an orgasm when he'd slipped one long, talented finger inside her, curving it to find and stroke the spot on the front, inside her... She'd looked at him and gasped, "Again?" He'd smiled that same smile, all the while his finger stroked against the magic spot he'd found, winding her up tighter and tighter. She'd cried out "again" just as she shattered a second time.

Every time he touched her, looked at her, something inside shifted, melted. She was ready to scream. How long could one wedding rehearsal take? And they still had the dinner to get through. It felt as if the night would never end. On the other hand, she was dreading that end. There was a sad pathetic part of her that wanted to spend as much time as possible with him, near him, because she had no idea how long it would be before she saw him again.

The really frightening part was she hadn't felt this alive in years. It was as if every sense, every part of her body had gone on red alert.

She retraced her steps to the lineup left of the altar and waited with the other bridesmaids until it was her turn—their turn. With a measured step she walked toward Eli with his smoldering eyes and his sensually chiseled mouth. The gleam in his eyes sent a shiver through her.

He held out his arm and she slipped hers through. Even through two layers of clothes—his and hers—the contact sizzled. A slick hot moisture gathered between her thighs and her nipples tightened, a purely instinctive response on a cellular level to the memory of the slide of his bare, hair-roughened skin against hers. It was as if she was programmed to respond to him with an intensity she could never know with another man.

Finally, mercifully, Mrs. Cantrell was content everyone could manage their way through the ceremony and they all headed to Lambert's, the nicest restaurant in Jackson Flats. Tara welcomed the bracing cold of the February night. It sobered her, helped her get her head back on straight.

The tables had been set up in a T formation. Greg, Lisa and their parents were all seated at the top part of the T, with the rest of the wedding party at a long table running perpendicular. Somehow, she wound up seated across from Eli, which was actually worse than if she'd been next to him.

Even though she, Traci and Mark Elliott were wrapped up in a discussion about Jackson Flats's town-square renovation—they were all committee members—only part of her brain was engaged. Every time she glanced up, she couldn't seem to avoid looking at Eli. She could feel his eyes on her, as if he couldn't ignore her, either.

"So, Eli, I understand you're a big dog now," Greg's father said as everyone was being served a shrimp-cocktail appetizer. Megaphone voices must run in the Waddell family, Tara assumed. Greg was as loud as anybody's business.

Eli nodded and his smile was different—it spoke of accomplishment, of a goal realized. "Yes, sir. I finished jump school today. I report to Fort Bragg on Monday for Special Forces training."

How had she not heard this? Everyone knew everyone else's business in small towns, especially one as small as Jackson Flats. Her belly clenched and an icy dread slid down her spine. "But that's dangerous, isn't it?" Tara blurted before she even stopped to think. It was one thing to know he was in the Army but Special Forces…

Eli shrugged his impossibly broad shoulders. "It's all a matter of perspective. What's dangerous is going into a situation you're not equipped to handle. But with the proper training—"

She interrupted him, cutting to the chase. "Will you be sent in to places where people are trying to kill you?" She knew he'd been stationed in Europe for a while but so far, he'd avoided being sent to Afghanistan or Iraq. Special Forces? That was about to change in a heartbeat.

"Easy, Tara," Greg said.

Tara held Eli's eyes and the entire table was quiet, waiting on his answer.

"Yes."

She nodded past the lump in her chest. "And Airborne Special Forces? That means you'll parachute into bad situations?"

He didn't have to answer, she saw it in his eyes. *Bad*

situations was giving it a positive spin. "Yeah," he admitted. "But hey, look at what inner-city cops face every day. Or firefighters like Danny." He nodded toward Greg's brother who sat halfway down the table. "It's really pretty much the same kind of deal. You train to handle what comes your way and then you go out and do it."

Danny nodded in silent acknowledgement and Tara caught the look that passed between Danny and Eli— a shared camaraderie of men who put their lives on the line every day in service to community and country.

He could've taken the opportunity to boast, to impress the table with the level of danger he could handle, but instead, he'd quietly deflected talk away from himself.

"I don't think I could jump out of a plane, and sure as hell not when some sucker's shooting at me." Greg whistled under his breath. "Man, you must have a set of brass ba—"

"Greg," Lisa cut him off with an elbow to his side. "Your mother. My mother."

Greg nodded in apology. "Sorry, Mrs. Mosley, Mom."

The rest of the table laughed and the tension lightened. Conversation began to flow around them again. Tara broke eye contact, her hand unsteady as she reached for her water glass, realizations washing over her. There was a part of her that wanted to scream *no, no, no don't do it, don't go to the Special Forces training*, and there was another part of her that felt as if she might burst with pride in his accomplishments, his discipline, his willingness to serve their country.

Underlying both those parts was the knowledge that she was sunk, lost, a goner. She'd sensed it the moment she saw him in his ROTC uniform ten years earlier. It was the reason she couldn't keep her panties on and her legs together at those other two weddings.

She was stupidly in love with Eli Murdoch.

5

IF HE COULD JUMP OUT OF A DAMN plane under enemy
fire, as Greg had pointed out, he could damn well go
for what he wanted with the one woman who was
driving him crazy. Time to man up.

Eli interrupted her as she was about to walk out the
door with a bridesmaid he didn't know. He snagged
Tara's arm. "Can I see you a minute, Tara?"

The other woman looked from Tara to him and back
again. "I'll see you later."

"Okay," she told Eli, while nodding for the other bridesmaid to go on without her. They stepped to the side,
out of the flow of traffic in and out of the restaurant.
She turned to face him, her lips slightly parted. Would
he ever get to the point that he didn't feel as if he was
slightly off balance every time she fixed those green
eyes on him? "You wanted me?"

That was an understatement.

Color washed her face. "I mean, what can I do for
you?"

He had a whole long list. It was one thing to decide
to keep his distance when she wasn't there. Now he

was having a damn hard time remembering why being with her was a bad idea.

"Can you give me a lift to my folks'?" he said.

For several long seconds she simply stood there, as if she was waging the same internal war he'd just fought.

"Sure. I can give you a ride."

Was there a look in her eyes or was it simply wishful thinking on his part? He wasn't going to waste time wondering. "Give me a minute to grab my duffel bag out of Greg's car."

Eli held the door open for her as they headed for the parking lot. She smiled at him over her shoulder. "Thanks. I'll warm up the car."

"Be right back."

He ran across the parking lot and waylaid Greg. "Hey, man, Tara's giving me a ride home."

"Okay. You know we're all heading over to Smokey Joe's around ten. Last night of freedom."

Eli was *so* not game for the strip-club scene. But he wasn't gonna stand in the parking lot and argue about it. "I'll give you a call later."

He made short work of getting back to Tara's Mini-Cooper. He tossed his duffel into the back, slammed the door and folded himself into the front passenger seat. Her scent wrapped around him before he even had the door closed. God, she was hot and he was hot for her.

James Otto's "Just Got Started Loving You" was

playing on the radio. The guy had that damn straight—one weekend with Tara wasn't going to be nearly enough, but it'd have to do.

Tara broke the silence. "Are the guys picking you up for the bachelor party?"

"I'm ducking out."

She slanted him a look as she pulled up to the Stop sign, her left blinker on. "I'd think after three weeks of training, you'd be honor bound to visit a strip club. Besides, it's a bachelor party."

She drove a manual and her hand gripped the gearshift knob. Eli reached between them and trailed his fingertip down the back of her hand, to the delicate bones of her wrist. He felt her tremble, or was that him? "*That's* not what I'm interested in."

Heat exploded in the air between them in shimmering waves. Damn, but it was always this way between them. His briefs were suddenly much, much tighter.

She caught the fullness of her lower lip in the edge of her teeth and then eased her tongue over the spot. She drew a deep breath, made her left turn and announced, "I'm going to exercise a woman's prerogative and change my mind."

What the hell? He'd overplayed his hand. "You're not going to give me a ride?"

She rolled to a stop at a red light and turned to him. "I can give you a ride to your parents'…or you can stay at my place." An I'm-gonna-rock-your-world promise curved her lips and gleamed in her eyes.

"There's room for your duffel bag at the end of my bed, Captain."

"Tara, are you sure?" What the hell was wrong with him? Why give her a chance to back out? Because she was more than he deserved after the way he'd treated her. He knew it had been a crappy thing not to contact her the last two years.

What the hell was he supposed to say? *The first time I wasn't ready for a relationship because I was just starting my military career and didn't want to be tied down? And the last time I woke up in bed with you, I realized I wanted to crawl inside your skin. It scared the hell out of me, so I ran?*

She leaned over, closing the gap between them and nibbled at the edge of his jaw, sending his pulse into orbit. "I've never been surer."

The traffic light turned green. "Then how far is it to your house? Because, baby, I can't kiss you the way I want to when you're driving. And I really, really want to kiss you."

She laughed, low and sexy. "I really, really want you to do a whole lot more than kiss me."

He realized he'd been waiting two years for that very thing.

6

Tara threw the car into park, killed the engine and turned to face the man she'd wanted for two long years, the man she'd loved for even longer, even if she'd never acknowledged it before. This time would be different. This time they had longer. A whole weekend. Still, she didn't dare touch him because the front seat of the Mini was too tight for sex. And once she touched him, they were going to have sex. "We're here."

"I'm not going to touch you until we get into your house because once I start, I'm not going to stop."

The low gravel of his voice and his words sent an express train of desire hurtling through her. They were *so* on the same page. She ached for his hands, his mouth, all of him on her, in her. "Grab your duffel bag and I'll unlock the kitchen door. It's closest."

Her hands were shaking so much she couldn't get the key in the lock. Eli came up behind her and wrapped his arm around her waist. His warm breath stirred against her shoulder, "Here, baby, let me."

She let him. She'd let him do anything.

And then they were in her house. He toed the door

closed and she turned in his arms. It was right where she wanted to be. Right where she belonged.

She wrapped her arms around the column of his neck and their mouths fused in a scorching kiss. His hunger, his frantic need matched hers. He cupped her breasts in his big hands through her thin sweater. She moaned into his mouth, pushing her breasts, her nipples harder into his hand. She slid one leg up his hip and wrapped it around his waist, bringing the bulge in his slacks into direct contact with her aching core.

It was as if he touched her in a place only he could, somewhere deep inside her, at the very center of her being. She tugged his shirt free of his pants and winnowed her hands beneath the material, plying her fingers over the sculpted muscles, his hot skin. He was so hard where a man should be hard—all over. Her warrior.

He tore his mouth from hers, his breathing ragged. "Where's the bedroom? If we don't move there now, I'm not gonna make it at all, Tara."

Here. Now. "Too far. I want you in every room before you leave." She was making memories. Once he left, she wanted to be able to remember making love to him, regardless of where she was in her house. "*Here* is a good place to start."

She relinquished her hold on him. She stepped out of her skirt and panties and tugged her sweater over her head, but left on her heels. He used to like heels. The hiss of his indrawn breath told her he still did. He dropped his pants and briefs and ripped his shirt off over his head, leaving him standing in her moonlit kitchen totally naked. He was leaner, harder than two years ago. His arousal jutted out from a thatch of dark curling hair below six-pack-ripped abs. His eyes glittered as he rolled on a condom…or at least tried to. It took him three tries to sheathe himself.

Tara lay back on the kitchen table, propping herself on her elbows. Eli wrapped his big hands around her thighs and leaned forward, his mouth finding hers, his erection nudging between her slick, ready folds.

And then he was inside her, stretching her, filling her, and she shifted up at the same time, using her feet to pull against his tight buns, taking him all the way home.

"Tara…oh, baby…so, so sweet…" He drew her eager nipple into his hot, warm mouth and she arched up off the table, into him.

"Eli—" She gasped his name as he suckled her. "Harder—" His teeth scraped against her sensitive tip even as he thrust into her. "Yes…yes…*yes.*"

She tightened around him, already halfway to finding her own release. She didn't say the words, but as she rocked with him she imbued each thrust with a silent *I love you*.

The first threads of an orgasm rippled through her. Eli threw his head back, pumping into her harder and faster. Claiming her. "Tara…Tara…Tara…" he roared as she spasmed around him.

He might not want it, but he owned her heart as well as her body.

7

DAMN! WHEN HAD HE EVER FELT SO good? He was stretched out facedown on Tara's soft flannel sheets and she was working some massage magic over his shoulders and back. Her sheets smelled like her. Spicy, sensual, his for now. The other two times they'd hooked up, it had been a Saturday night and they'd only had a few short hours. This was different. They had time. They had all weekend, except for the hours they were obliged to be at the wedding.

This was so much better than a hotel. Her house was a lot like he'd come to think of her—earthy, yet sensual.

"Relax, soldier-boy," she said, her fingers working at a knotted muscle. Damn, but it was sexy the irreverent way she called him that.

"You're a woman of hidden talents," Eli murmured.

She stroked across his shoulders, a soothing rhythm. "We lived with my aunt for a while when I was about twelve. She was a masseuse and she taught me a lot."

He could get used to this. He'd had a massage once before but it hadn't felt like this. Tara's touch was magic. "You were obviously a good student."

She laughed softly. "I thought you might enjoy getting pampered after spending the last three weeks jumping out of planes."

"Everything you do feels good." He'd never been the possessive type but a sudden thought speared him. He didn't want her making any other guy feel good. Right. She was supposed to wait around for him to show up every two years or so and sleep with her? He couldn't see that working for her, but he didn't want to think about some other guy stretched out on her bed. Or plunging into her on her kitchen table.

She slid her hands down his spine and began to knead his ass. "Flattery will get you everywhere."

In the kitchen, his cell phone went off. "Damn. That's probably Greg, wondering why I haven't shown up at the bachelor party."

Her hands stilled. "Do you want to go?"

He rolled to his back. She was serious. "Woman, why in the hell would I want to go to a strip joint when everything I want is right here." He circled her nipple with his fingertip and watched it harden at his touch.

A slow smile curved her mouth and lit her eyes. "*That* was the right answer." She leaned forward and kissed him. Slow, long, deep.

His phone went off again. Tara sat back and laughed. "I think you better tell him you're unavailable."

Eli sat up and swung his legs over the mattress's edge and then paused. "You know Greg isn't exactly discreet. Everyone in Jackson Flats will know I stayed here tonight before Greg and Lisa even get to saying their I do's tomorrow."

She wrapped her arms around him from behind, her bare breasts pressed against his back, and kissed his shoulder, her hair a silken slide against his skin. "Does that bother you?" she asked.

"I'm a big boy—"

She slipped her hand around his waist and wrapped her fingers around him. "Yes, you are." She stroked him. "Just one of the things I like about you," she said before releasing him with a naughty laugh.

He grinned but continued. "I'm heading to Bragg on Sunday. But you live here and you're a schoolteacher. I don't want you to catch shit because I can't keep my hands off you."

She rubbed her breasts in a circular motion against his back. "I'm not too good at the hands-off business, either." She nipped an erotic path against the back of his neck. "Don't worry. Do you really think I care if people know I'm doing my best to wear you out before you leave?"

"Oh? Is that the plan? You know, I've trained for a high level of endurance. Do you really think you *can* wear me out?"

"I don't know…but it sure will be fun to find out, won't it?" The vixen took her foot, put it on his ass and, with a quick thrust, shoved him off the bed. "For goodness' sake, go call Greg. And hurry back. I've got a mission to accomplish."

He hurried.

8

"WAKE UP, SLEEPYHEAD," Eli whispered in her ear the next morning.

It took a second for Tara to realize she wasn't in the middle of some wickedly good dream. She blinked her eyes open and gave an inner sigh of contentment at finding his sexy, beard-stubbled face next to hers. It should be against the law for a man to look that good first thing in the morning, or anytime. Eli was, plain and simple, too hot.

"Morning," she said. And then she noted a marked absence of sunlight at the bedroom window. "What time is it?" His finely sculpted chest and shoulders were blocking her view of the clock.

"O-seven-hundred hours."

"Seven in the morning?" If it were anyone but him, she'd groan and roll back over. She didn't like to get up early on the weekend, but he was here for such a short time, sleep really didn't matter, did it? She reached out and skimmed her fingers over his bare, hair-smattered forearm simply because she could. She loved to touch him. She loved to look at him. "What time did you get up?"

"I get up every morning at 0500," he said, smoothing her hair back from her face in an intimate gesture.

"That's obscene." She couldn't hold back a groan. He made her feel like a veritable garden slug.

He grinned. "That's discipline, baby. I've already gone for a six-mile run."

"Show-off. Although there probably wasn't anyone up to see." She noticed the dark stain on his T-shirt that she'd missed earlier. She wasn't the most observant human being on the planet first thing in the morning. "So that's why you're kind of sweaty."

He shook his head and gave her an indulgent smile, as if he thought she was too cute and too sexy all rolled into one. Hey, he could look at her like that all day, any day. "I made breakfast for us," he said.

She sighed. "You're not a man, you're a god."

"You'd better wait until you've eaten my cooking to decide."

"Do you always…" She petered out. Her brain definitely wasn't fully functional or she would've never started that line of questioning. Did she really want to know if he did this for other women? That was a resounding no.

As his gaze tangled with hers, he reached up and tucked her hair behind her ear. The tenderness behind that gesture stole her breath. "No," he said. "I don't. You're the first." His gaze didn't waver and she glimpsed an unexpected vulnerability in her big bad paratrooper. "That massage last night, do you…"

It was gratifying. He didn't want to think about her doing those things for some other guy any more than she wanted him preparing breakfast for another woman. "No. Never before like that. You're the first, too."

"Give me a minute and I'll bring you breakfast in bed."

"You don't have to—"

He stopped her with a finger to her lips. "I want to."

She hurried to the bathroom to take care of morning business while he headed back to the kitchen. If you skipped the part where he disappeared for years at a time without a word, he was damn near perfect. His being gone for years at a time, however, was sort of problematic.

He sauntered back in, bearing a laden tray. He'd lost the sweaty T-shirt along the way and the bulge of his biceps, the cut of his pecs, the ripple of his abs all gave her a totally different kind of hunger.

He sat on the edge of the bed and placed the lap tray between them. A mountain of eggs, half a rasher of bacon, buttered toast and coffee were on the tray. Was he crazy? "I can't possibly eat all this."

"I'll share it with you," he said with a grin, picking up a fork. "Remember, babe, you've got to keep your strength up." The look in his eyes set her internal temperature soaring. "So, you lived with an aunt when you were a kid? Just you or your whole family?"

"My whole family is me and my mom." She nibbled at a piece of crisp bacon.

"What about your dad?"

"My parents divorced when I was three. Louis—" she hadn't called him Dad since she'd had a choice in what to call him "—remarried and his new wife didn't want to be bothered with a stepkid. My mother's way of forgetting about the divorce was to crisscross the great state of Tennessee. We never lived anywhere longer than six months…until we got here."

A frown drew his dark brows together. "So, your mom decided to settle down in Jackson Flats?"

"No, I decided to settle down in Jackson Flats. There was something about here that spoke to me. I'd always wanted a place that belonged to me, where it felt as if I belonged. I don't know what it was about Jackson Flats, but we hadn't been here long before I knew this was what I'd been looking for. It offered me the roots I'd always craved."

"And look at you now. An upstanding citizen, a home owner, a teacher—fully vested in the community. I heard you talking over dinner about the town-square renovation."

"That's me." Firmly settled in Jackson Flats. "When did you know you wanted to join the service?" It was the first really personal question she'd ever asked him.

"I can't remember a time when I didn't know. My grandfather was a career military man and I grew up hearing his stories. I've always known it was my duty to serve my country."

"And Special Forces?"

"I'm good at what I do, Tara. But I wasn't challenged anymore. Joining Special Forces makes me a more valuable asset to the military."

She nodded. She didn't like it, but she knew where he was coming from. "It notches up your ability to serve."

"Exactly."

She shifted some eggs on the plate with her fork. "It doesn't leave a whole lot of room for relationships, does it?"

His look was direct, open, honest. "It can be done, but it takes a special kind of woman. Orders come down as alerts and you're gone. You can't tell where you're going, mainly because you don't know, yourself. Most women find it too hard to take."

And that was that. She had her answer. Still, she had plenty of time after he left to be depressed. She refused to waste the time she had with him now. Scooting over on the mattress, she pulled his T-shirt she'd slept in over her head and tossed it to the floor.

"Well, you might not know where you're going on your next assignment, but I know where I'd like you to go now."

9

ELI LISTENED AS GREG AND LISA exchanged their vows, but he couldn't seem to look anywhere except at Tara. Her gaze held his. She hid nothing from him, or from anyone else who might glance at the two of them instead of at the bride and groom.

She loved him.

She hadn't spoken the words aloud, but he realized it had been in her touch. Her eyes proclaimed it, even as they asked nothing in return.

He felt humbled by her generosity. What had he ever done to deserve someone as special as Tara? Special didn't begin to describe her. He'd never felt for another woman what he felt for her. But there was no room in his life for a relationship now. And after he finished his training, what kind of relationship could he offer a woman who'd finally put down deep roots in Jackson Flats? If he made her a military wife, could he bear to watch that life change her? He'd be sent out and she'd spend more and more time alone at whatever base he was stationed at. What would happen when loneliness took its toll and the look in her eyes turned from love to bitterness? What kind of man would he be to drag her down that path simply because he couldn't bear the thought of being away from her? A selfish bastard, that's what he'd be.

"I now pronounce you man and wife," the preacher said. "You may kiss your bride."

Three minutes later, he and Tara were heading down the aisle together and he couldn't help feeling there was something right about having her on his arm. "Have I told you how beautiful you look in that dress?" he asked in an undertone as they cleared the church doors.

"Not in the last half hour," she said with a sassy smile.

"Only because of that vow business. Otherwise, I would've. The only thing better than you in that dress is—"

"Hey, Tara," a big blond guy with a toothy smile interrupted them, moving forward to envelope her in a bear hug. "I wanted to tell you you're looking good. Maybe we could do a movie one day next week."

Translate to "maybe I could do you one day next week." Eli bristled with a nearly overwhelming urge to kick this guy's ass.

"Jack, this is Captain Eli Murdoch. Eli, Coach Jack Thompson."

The guy was pretty big, but Eli was taller and fitter. He looked down at the other man. "Coach? Really? Peewee football?"

Next to Eli, Tara made a choking sound.

It was Jack's turn to bristle. "High school. Varsity.

State champs two years running." He smiled and turned his attention back to Tara. "I'll give you a call next week."

"Um…okay."

Jack walked away and Eli said to her, "I don't like him."

"Really? You could have fooled me." She laughed. "Peewee football? Eli."

He didn't see what was so damn funny. "Did you go out with him?"

She nodded. "Last year. We dated for a while."

She was too casual. She'd slept with the son of a bitch. "I knew I didn't like him."

"Ancient history," she said, running her fingers up his arm and leaning into him, her voice low in his ear, her scent all around him, her breath a warm seduction against his jaw. "The reception is going to last at least two hours," she said.

"Two hours is a long time. A lot can happen in two hours."

Her eyes had that wicked twinkle that always portended good things to come. "A whole lot can happen in two hours…if you're not at a wedding reception." Her hip brushed against his thigh and she had his full attention. "Do you think anyone would notice if we slipped away?"

"I'm fairly certain they would," he said. "But I couldn't care less. Let's go home."

10

TARA DIDN'T WANT TO FALL asleep and waste precious time. She'd never felt so content. She realized that much as she liked her little house, it had never felt like home the way it did now that Eli was here. He felt like home to her.

She propped on her elbow and studied the play of firelight over Eli's nakedness. Even if he wasn't the most beautiful man on the planet—in a totally masculine way—she'd still love him for his quiet strength of character, his devilish smile, his sense of humor—

He reached up and cupped her jaw in his hand, his thumb brushing against her cheek. "What are you thinking?"

She drew in a deep breath and said without prevarication, "That even if you weren't the most beautiful man on the planet, I'd still love you."

He grew very still. The moment for an *I love you, too* came and went. She wasn't surprised. She hadn't really expected...

"Tara—"

"It's okay, Eli. I just wanted you to know before you

left." She caught his hand in hers and kissed his fingertips. "When you're training, when you're on assignment, just know that I love you." She laughed. "I think I fell in love with you the moment I saw you. It was my first day at Jackson Flats High and you were in your ROTC uniform." He looked sort of funny and she knew it was because he totally didn't recall seeing her. "I know. You didn't even know I was alive until you came back home for that first wedding."

He grimaced and looked apologetic. "True. I'm sorry. You were younger than me and well, I just didn't notice." He pressed an openmouthed kiss to her shoulder and a lazy heat spiraled through her. "But I made up for it in spades. When you walked into that church, it was like taking a kick to the gut. It's still that way every damn time you walk into a room."

He might not love her the way she loved him, but at least she wasn't totally alone in this thing between them. "Good."

He laughed and then sobered. "I was just starting out in the military. There wasn't any room in my life for entanglements."

She waited. What about two years ago?

He nodded. She hadn't even had to pose the question. Increasingly, this weekend, it seemed as if they were more and more tuned in to each other's thoughts. Eli continued, "The last time we were together, I woke up that morning scared to death."

Over the last two years she'd replayed every moment

they'd ever spent together. What was he talking about? "Why? Did I say something?" Then she decided to take another approach. "Did I look that bad first thing in the morning?" she asked lightly.

There wasn't even a glimmer of humor in his eyes. "The way it was with you…the way it is when we're together… It's never been like that with anyone else." It wasn't exactly an oath of undying devotion, but Tara's heart sang to know he, at least, felt that there was more between them than just sex. It was a start, a jumping-off point. "I'm not proud of it, but I ran. I'm sure you thought I was a bastard not to write or call."

"The thought crossed my mind—a couple of times."

He winced. "I'm not great at keeping in touch, just ask my mother—"

Tara laughed aloud at the idea of walking up to Mrs. Murdoch and asking her about Eli's correspondence habits. "I think I'll pass."

He offered a half smile. "Okay, maybe not. But my mother would like you. I'll e-mail…and I'll call when I can."

"You know, I'd like that." And she'd have to be content with that. "And I know what you'd like."

"You do, do you?"

"Uh-huh." She knelt over him and followed the contour of his chest with her lips, kissing him, her tongue darting over his nipples.

"Oh, yes, you do…" His words ended on a groan as

she moved down the hard, ridged plane of his belly. He buried his hand in her hair and tugged.

"Easy, soldier-boy, I'm going to get here…eventually."

"If you don't kill me first."

"Oh, I have no intention of killing you…but I fully intend to make things hard."

"Have a look, babe. Mission accomplished."

11

"THANKS FOR GIVING ME A RIDE to the airport," Eli said, sitting beside Tara as her Mini Cooper ate up the highway.

"You know I wanted to."

It wasn't just her blond hair, green eyes and hot body that made her beautiful. She was generous and loving, but at the same time she gave as good as she got. He figured she was pretty much the perfect woman. "You're a helluva woman, Tara Swenson."

"It's about time you figured that out, soldier-boy." She kept her eyes trained on the highway in front of her. "I should tell you something. Something I just figured out myself this morning."

"Okay?"

"Remember I told you I hadn't been here long when I figured out Jackson Flats was where I belonged?"

"Yeah?"

"It wasn't the 'where,' it was the 'who.' It wasn't Jackson Flats that called to me. It was the day I saw you for the first time that I knew I was home. My roots are with you," she finally said, laying her soul bare to him.

Yeah, that's what she said now, but how would she feel when she was alone on a military base while he was halfway around the world for a couple of weeks or even months? He cleared his throat. "I'll be better about keeping in touch this time."

"It would be impossible to be worse."

She obviously wasn't happy with his reaction, but what the hell did she expect from him? He was trying to do the honorable thing.

"I love you, Eli, but I'm not going to wait on you forever. I've got to have more of you than a quick fling every couple of years."

Point taken, but he was working with limited options. "Tara, I told you I'd write."

"Look, you might be Captain Murdoch to your men, but you're not in charge of me, so don't use that patronizing tone. Do you know what courage is, Captain? It's wading into the fray when you're scared shitless. You know you're about to be shot down, but you go there anyway." Okay. He got her analogy. She'd had the guts to lay out to him how she felt. "Maybe you can find your balls while you're in Special Forces training. Maybe when they finish with you, you'll actually have the guts to admit you love me, too."

Goddamn straight she wasn't one of his men. They'd never talk to him like that. "Are you through?"

"Almost." Damn her. Even when she'd pissed him off and she was radiating hostility, she was still sexy. "I might have been too stupid to realize I loved you, but good Lord, I finally did. You, on the other hand, are too scared to even consider the possibility. God help us both."

A tight, tense silence stretched between them. Who the hell did she think she was? He jumped out of planes. He was about to become one of the deadliest forces in the U.S. Army and she, a schoolteacher from Jackson Flats, Tennessee, was going to tell him he needed to find out what courage was? He was so goddamn angry he couldn't even begin to find the cool detachment that served him so well in his job.

"You can just drop me off at the curb," he said in the terse, clipped tone that always let his men know they'd crossed a line.

"I was planning to."

He should've known she'd have to have the last word. Tara pulled over and he got out of the car without a word. Reaching into the backseat, he yanked out his duffel.

"Eli."

"Yes?"

"I love you. Take care of yourself."

He straightened and slammed the door. Then he was pissed because he felt like a jerk. He turned and made his way through the automatic airport doors.

What the hell was wrong with him? He was so angry he could…what? He'd never had anger issues, but Tara had pushed him too far… His steps faltered. By speaking the truth.

He'd run like hell two years ago and he was still running, too much of a chickenshit to bare his soul. He could learn a lesson or two in bravery from this woman.

He pulled out his cell phone and dialed the number she'd programmed in for him last night. He sprinted back toward the front of the airport.

"Tara, it's Eli. You've got to come back. I forgot something."

He burst through the double doors and she was standing at the curb where she'd dropped him off. He clicked the phone off.

She dropped her cell into her pocket, her eyes never leaving his face. "I never left. What'd you forget?"

He manned up and stepped forward, bracketing her face in his hands. "The one thing I can't live without. You. I love you, Tara."

She wrapped her arms around his neck, tears shimmering in her eyes. "It's about time you figured that out, soldier-boy."

Epilogue

Six months later…

"HEY, BABY, DO YOU THINK anyone would notice if we disappeared now that the wedding ceremony is over?" Eli asked, his breath stirring tendrils of hair near her ear, setting off the usual three-alarm fire inside her that occurred whenever he was near.

"Since we're the main attraction, I think they might," Tara said, leading him to where their guests waited to congratulate them. Eli's buddy, the tall dark and aloof Lieutenant Colonel Mitch Dugan had served as his best man and stood apart, the first in line to congratulate them. Mitch wasn't exactly warm and fuzzy but he was a nice guy and at least she'd know one person when she moved into her new home at Fort Bragg.

"No regrets?" Eli asked softly. It was uncanny the way they seemed to know what was going through one another's heads.

All her worldly possessions sat packed in a U-Haul van, ready for the trip to North Carolina. She'd close on her house—the first place she'd ever called her own—on Thursday. She'd expected at least a momentary twinge of sadness at giving up everything, but there hadn't been even a flicker. She was simply excited to be with Eli.

"None. If home is where the heart is, my home will always be with you."

* * * * *

Turn the page for a sneak preview of

Who Needs Mistletoe?

*Sophie Madigan practically drools when her
last-minute client walks in on Christmas Eve.
Wealthy Trey Shelton III has bedroom eyes, a wicked
grin and a body to die for! And Sophie can't think
of any Christmas gift she'd enjoy more…*

by Kate Hoffmann

THE ARTIFICIAL CHRISTMAS TREE looked even tackier than it had the previous year, the plastic pine needles worn thin in spots and the wire branches drooping. Sophie Madigan hung the last of the ornaments on a high bough, then stepped back, forcing a smile. "Doesn't that look festive, Papa?"

She glanced over her shoulder at her father, who sat at the huge desk in their parlor, his reading glasses perched on the end of his nose, aviation manuals and charts spread out in front of him. He nodded distractedly, then took another sip of his whiskey. It was barely noon and he had already poured himself a drink, Sophie mused.

"I should have bought some new lights," she continued. "Half of these are burned out."

"Looks fine, darlin'," he murmured, without even looking up.

Sophie sighed and began to gather the boxes and bags strewn over the plank floor. Why did she even bother? Trying to celebrate Christmas in the middle of the South Pacific was a lost cause. She remembered Christmases past, when she and her parents had traveled to places where entire towns had been decorated, places where it actually snowed.

Outside their small house on the tiny Polynesian island of Taratea, the trade winds kept the temperatures at a constant eighty-three degrees and the wet season made the air thick with humidity. The heady scent of tiare and hibiscus and frangipani seeped through the shutters that lined the lanai and she could hear the soft patter of raindrops on the tin roof. Sometimes it seemed as if it would never stop raining.

Sophie had hoped to spend this Christmas with her mother in Paris. But for the third year in a row, she'd reluctantly refused the invitation, choosing instead to stay with her father, Jack "Madman" Madigan. Christmas in Paris would have been a happy affair. Her uncles and aunts were all excellent cooks and there would have been food, followed by gifts, followed by more food.

When she broached the subject of spending the holidays in Paris, her father had told her to go. But as the time to leave got closer, Sophie saw him sink further and further into a deep depression. He had no one except her. No family, few friends. Since his eyesight had gone bad, he'd cut himself off from nearly everyone.

Sophie turned away from the tree and crossed the room, peering over her father's shoulder. "What are you working on?"

He had a map of the Society Islands spread out in front of him and he was studying a small archipelago through a magnifying glass, squinting to see the fine print. Her father's eyesight had been failing for nearly five years. It had become so bad, he'd been grounded, prohibited from doing what he did best.

Since then, Sophie had been forced to take over his air-charter operation, making almost daily flights between Tahiti and any one of the fourteen inhabited islands nearby. To make ends meet, they'd sold off four of the five planes to pay her father's debts. With one small plane left and only one pilot—Sophie herself—they made just enough to get by.

Sophie had tried to convince her father to sell the last plane and move back to the States where he could get medical care and she could get a better-paying job, but Jack held out hope that his eyesight would suddenly return and he'd be back in business. "Are we going on a trip?"

"I'm mapping out a flight plan for you for tomorrow," he murmured.

"I didn't know I had a charter," Sophie said, frowning. "Papa, tomorrow is Christmas Eve. Don't you think we could take the day off, maybe do a little celebrating? The tree is up. I thought I might make a nice dinner and we could open our gifts and maybe even listen to some Christmas music."

"This guy is willing to pay ten thousand American for three days' worth of flying. I didn't think it was a job you'd want to refuse."

She gasped. *"Ten thousand* dollars? For three days' work?"

Jack nodded, then handed her a slip of paper. "His name is Peter Shelton. He's some bigwig for the Shelton Hotel chain. They're looking for a new location to build some fancy-schmancy new resort and they want to buy a whole island, make it real exclusive. You need to meet him at eight tomorrow morning at Faaa. At the hangar."

Sophie stared down at the name and phone number written on the scrap of paper. *"Quelle chance,"* she murmured. "Peter Shelton. Shelton Hotels." He sounded like a pretty important guy. Anyone who worked on Christmas Eve and paid more than three thousand dollars a day for a charter had to be important. "Why would he choose us?"

"Probably because no one else would take the job on Christmas Eve," Jack replied. "Here," he said, pointing to the map. "Fly him up here to this little atoll. There's a nice-size island with a decent lagoon."

"Suaneva? Didn't they try to build a resort there once?"

"About thirty years ago. But the developer ran out of money. The lagoon is a little tight for landing and taking off, but a good pilot should be able to get in and out. Hell, if he decides to build there, I can fly his workers in and out. We'll haul freight, and later the guests. We could work out an exclusive long-term contract and maybe buy a few new planes. I want you to really impress this guy, Sophie girl. Make him see that a partnership with Madigan Air would be good for both of us."

Sophie rested her hand on his shoulder. "Yes, Papa." She knew it was all just a pipe dream. Or maybe he did expect her to spend the rest of her life flying for him. She'd found a doctor in Sydney who'd promised a simple but expensive surgery for her father's sight problems, but when she'd mentioned this to him, Jack had completely discounted the option, preferring to stick to the herbal remedies a local *tahua* woman had prescribed.

Besides, it wasn't as if they had the money for the operation. Though ten thousand American dollars would go a long way toward paying for it, it still wasn't enough. Sooner or later, she'd have to accept the fact her life was here, caring for her father and eking out a living for them both as best she could.

She glanced around the small *fare* they called home. Built onto a hillside overlooking the water and perched on stilts, the interior of the cottage was small, just enough room for a few bedrooms and a parlor. But most of their living was done outside, on the wide lanai that circled the house.

Tourists would say she was living in paradise, but to Sophie, it often felt like a prison. Unable to enjoy the beauty that surrounded her, she longed for the excitement of living in a city, the noise and the people, never knowing what was around the next corner.

Slipping out of the house, she walked across the

small lawn to a point that overlooked the bay. People paid thousands of dollars to come and admire a view like this, she mused. The steeply raked crags covered with lush vegetation, the turquoise water and white sand, the little *fare*, surrounded with flowering vines and bushes.

Perhaps she might convince her father to sell and find a place in Pape'ete. Maybe then she could meet some people her own age, maybe even find a man to distract her from her troubles. She flopped down onto the lawn and stared up at the sky, the dampness from the rain soaking through her pareu.

Though she was emotionally exhausted, something inside her couldn't seem to rest. She felt as though she was ready to jump out of her skin. She smoothed her hands over her body and closed her eyes as the rain pelted her face. The sensations her hands evoked were enough to remind her how long it had been since she'd been touched by another.

It had been nearly a year since she'd enjoyed the pleasures a man's body offered. Though her Irish-American father would be more than happy if she decided to enter a convent, her French mother had given Sophie a very practical and healthy attitude about sex. One must accept that a woman has desires, her mother had told her, and they must be fulfilled. There is no sin in acting upon these feelings. As long as both parties agree there will be no promises the next morning.

After she finished flying Peter Shelton around the